The Kids Get Horses

Stu Campbell

ISBN: 978-0-9962019-8-8

6   5   4   3   2   1

Edited by Mira Perrizo
Cover and text design by D.K. Luraas
Cover painting by Larry Jones, Bouse, Arizona

Printed in the United States of America

Contents

A Good Start

Jimmy McIntyre got back to the Rehabilitation Ranch. He'd bought some saddles, bridles, halters, blankets, and pads at the horse sale and even managed to buy one horse. He also bought a carton of good, heavy leather gloves. Jimmy and Craig unloaded the horse and Craig fed the horses while Jimmy unloaded the tack. Emily went to the house and started to fix supper.

After supper, Jimmy outlined his plans to Craig and Emily for the time remaining before Mason brought the new "clients" out.

"We'll need to build some new saddle racks for the saddles we bought today," said Jimmy. "I think we've got enough material. According to Mister Mason, we'll be having some more youngsters arriving in a few days. Craig, you'll be depended on to set an example with these new youngsters when they arrive. Can you do that?"

"I think so," answered Craig.

"Good! I'll plan on it! Are you ready to move into the bunkhouse? You'll be the first occupant in there, see to it that it's clean for our new arrivals. Emily, do you have enough groceries for extra mouths for a few days?"

"Yes," replied Emily. "How many kids are coming?"

"Youngsters," corrected Jimmy. "We need to treat these people as young adults. I don't know how many are coming. We'll find out when they arrive. Make up plenty of food and we'll survive on leftovers if necessary. Also, Mister Mason indicated that we're going to get some young mustangs in a day or two. We'll have plenty to keep the youngsters busy."

The next day, Jimmy and Craig built some new saddle racks out of old material. When they were done, Jimmy saddled the new horse and rode him around the corral to see what he'd bought. When he was satisfied that the horse was what he thought he was, he told Craig to saddle his horse and they'd ride over to the Burkharts to see when they'd need some help hauling hay.

The ride over to the Burkhart's place was pleasant and Jimmy decided that he'd made a good purchase with the horse he'd bought. They found Richard Burkhart baling hay south of the ranch house.

"Got another horse, huh," said Burkhart, as he shut off the tractor. "Hello Craig."

Jimmy thought it was nice that Burkhart acknowledged Craig each time they met. Jimmy thought, *All too often, juvenile delinquents are ignored when in the company of adults.*

"Hello Mister Burkhart," replied Craig. "How are you doing today?"

Jimmy also thought, *Craig's reply was proper. Maybe we are making a difference.*

When Jimmy had first met Burkhart, Burkhart impressed him as being a gruff, antisocial individual. When he'd got to know him a little better, he found out that his first impression was wrong. Burkhart was gruff, almost to the point of being antisocial, but the true individual was really quite nice. It just took a little time to get to know him.

"When do you figure you'll be ready to haul hay?" asked Jimmy, getting right to the point. Burkhart had impressed him as being a direct sort of person.

"I should be ready tomorrow. Do you want to come over and help?"

"That's the idea," replied Jimmy. "We've got more youngsters coming and I'm sure we'll need something to do to keep them busy."

Showing some apprehension, Burkhart asked, "How many kids you got coming?"

"I don't know just yet. Mason hasn't informed me. Right now, we've got room for nine more youngsters in the bunkhouse."

"I'd appreciate the help," said Burkhart. "I'm still having some trouble with this foot healing right and don't get along very good."

"We'll be here tomorrow."

"Good," replied Burkhart as he started the tractor, indicating that the visit was over.

Jimmy and Craig turned their horses back toward the Juvenile Rehabilitation Ranch. Craig waved as they left and Burkhart returned the wave.

Jimmy didn't know what to expect when the new arrivals showed up. He wondered if they were already becoming hard-core criminals, gang members, or just some kids that got off on the wrong foot and needed a fresh start. *Oh well,* he thought, *whatever they are, they'll get a chance to get a new start here.*

"What are you thinking about?" asked Craig.

"Just wondering what the youngsters coming are going to be like," answered Jimmy. "It'll be interesting to see how these young juvenile delinquents get along with the young mustangs."

The following day, Jimmy and Craig went to the Burkharts to help haul hay. That evening, after a day of hauling hay, a truck arrived with eight young mustangs. Jimmy, Craig, and Emily went out to meet the truck. The colts were all old enough to be weaned and they looked scared when they entered the corral from the truck.

As Jimmy and the truck driver watched the colts, Jimmy asked, "What can you tell me about these colts?"

"Nothing, really," said the driver. "They've never been handled. They've been in a corral at the BLM holding corrals."

"That's okay," said Jimmy.

Craig approached and asked, "Can I go in there and catch one?"

"I doubt if you can catch one," said Jimmy. "But you can try. Be careful! They don't know what your intentions are and their self-preservation is foremost in their minds."

Emily came down from the house. "They're so cute. Don't get hurt, Craig," she said as Craig entered the corral.

The colts were milling around and as Craig entered the corral, their milling became more frantic. Seeing this, Jimmy said, "Go to the middle of the corral and just stand there. Let them get used to your presence."

Craig did as he was told and soon the colts settled down. They weren't completely comfortable, but they circled around him, warily watching him. One of the colts started to approach him.

"Just stand there," said Jimmy softly. "He's curious."

The colt took another step or two in Craig's direction, alert to any move this strange human might make.

"I think he likes me," said Craig.

At the sound of Craig's voice, the colt wheeled and ran to the safety of the other colts.

"What happened?" asked Craig.

"Your voice scared him," answered Jimmy. Then he added humorously, "Maybe he doesn't understand English yet."

"That's all right," said Emily. "There's no harm done and the colt still has a lot of time to learn."

"Let's let them get used to the place," said Jimmy. "We'll feed out in the middle of the corral. Just being in among them will do a lot to help get them acclimated."

"Anything else you need from me?" asked the truck driver.

"Do you have any papers or a brand inspection to show that we have the colts legally?"

"Oh yes, I almost forgot," said the driver, reaching into his pocket. As he handed the papers to Jimmy, he said, "Call me when you have them halter broke. I'll come pick them up and bring you a new bunch. I've been told what this deal is all about and I hope it works, not only for the colts, but for the kids as well."

"We'll see who benefits the most," said Jimmy. "You want to spend the night?"

"No," said the truck driver, "I told my wife I'd be home tonight. It'll be late, but I'd better be there."

"Suit yourself," said Jimmy.

The following day, the new arrivals hadn't showed up and Craig and Jimmy went to the Burkhart Ranch to help haul hay when their chores were done. When they got there, the Burkharts were just finishing breakfast.

"Get enough breakfast this morning, Craig?" Burkhart asked. "You'll need it today."

"Yes sir," replied Craig.

They started toward the tractor and trailer. "The Missus," said Burkhart, "can drive. I'll stack and you boys can throw the bales to me."

Jimmy felt some resentment about being referred to as a boy but rationalized it by thinking, *He's referring to Craig and me. And he is quite a bit older than us.* Ignoring his own resentment, he said, "That sounds like a plan."

While they were unloading the second load of hay for the morning, Emily came riding up on the horse Burkhart had given her.

"Need a hand?" she asked, as she got off the horse.

"Women aren't supposed to work in the hay," said Jimmy, jokingly.

"But you have Louise here," replied Emily.

"Louise is leaving directly to fix a noon meal," said Mrs. Burkhart.

"Then I'll fill in," said Emily.

"You didn't come out here to haul hay," said Jimmy. "What brings you out here?"

"I thought the ride might be a nice change of pace," said Emily, teasing. "Oh, yes, Mister Mason called. He's bringing out some boys tomorrow. He should be here by nine o'clock."

"How many?"

"He said he's bringing five. They'll have their stuff and be ready to stay."

Jimmy turned to Burkhart. "I won't be able to show up tomorrow because of the new youngsters coming. I need to be there when they arrive. But I'll send Craig over. That might help some."

"It'll help a lot," said Burkhart. "How will he get here? Do you want me to come over and get him?"

"I'll send him over in the truck," said Jimmy. "He'll be here early enough to put in a good day's work." Jimmy watched Craig's reaction as he told that to Burkhart. Craig didn't have a reaction.

When they'd finished hauling hay for the day and were driving back to the Rehabilitation Ranch, Craig asked Jimmy, "Aren't you afraid I'll take the truck and run off?"

"Not really," replied Jimmy. "You'd break the trust I've put in you, and I've got a lot of faith and trust in you. I don't think you would, anyway."

"What if I did?"

"Well, you wouldn't get far with that state insignia on each door. Besides that, you don't have a driver's license. You'll be going the way we ride our horses over—you won't be on the road. If you did run off, when you got caught, and you would get caught, you wouldn't come back here, you'd go straight to reform school."

"I guess I can do that," replied Craig.

"Run off or go to reform school?" asked Jimmy, trying hard to hold back a laugh.

"I haven't figured that out yet," said Craig, not trying at all to hold back a laugh.

The next day, Craig drove over to the Burkharts, alone. He had a stern reminder from Jimmy, "Don't be late!"

Jimmy watched him drive off and said to Emily, "I really hope I'm not putting too much trust in him too early."

"He'll be all right," said Emily. "I think he's made a lot of progress just in the time I've been here."

"I hope you're right," said Jimmy.

Jimmy made an inspection of the bunkhouse while he was waiting for Mason to show up. He decided Craig might need a little prompting on his housekeeping. There were just a few things scattered around the room.

Mason was late showing up and didn't arrive until about ten

thirty. When he arrived, he had four youngsters with him. In another car was Doctor Peterson, the psychologist.

"You're late," said Jimmy to Mason.

"We had some problems with one of the boys and had to return him," said Mason.

"Problems?" queried Jimmy.

"Yes, but nothing you want to concern yourself with. These are the first residents," said Mason as he introduced him to the youngsters. "This is William Pierce, this is Clyde Hollingsworth, this is David Brewster and this is Michael Thornton. Gentlemen, this is Jimmy McIntyre, manager of this ranch. You'll be responsible to him. You've all been told what's expected of you and Jimmy will be supervising you. There's another youngster here—by the way Jimmy, where is Craig?"

"He's over at the Burkharts hauling hay," answered Jimmy. "I sent him over this morning."

Mason looked a little surprised. "We'll discuss that later," he said.

Ignoring Mason's look of surprise, Jimmy walked over and shook hands with each of the youngsters. As he did so he asked each boy if he had a nickname.

"I'm Bill," said William.

"I'm Holly," said Clyde.

"Short for Hollingsworth?" asked Jimmy. Jimmy immediately thought of Honey at the Wilson Ranch and how he'd gotten used to his nickname. He thought this youngster might be having some trouble with it.

"Yeah," replied the youngster.

"I'm Shorty," said David.

Jimmy could see how Shorty got his nickname. He was a full head shorter than the others.

"I'm Mike," said Michael.

"Gentlemen," said Jimmy, "I will try to remember your nicknames, but I make no guarantees. We're not too formal around here so you call me Jimmy. The bunkhouse is over there, get your stuff and we'll get you settled in. Craig is already moved in, you can have any bunks you wish other than his."

Doctor Peterson came over as the boys moved their stuff into the bunkhouse. He had some papers with him. "You can look these over when you get a chance," he said, as he handed the papers to Jimmy. "There's a file on each one of these youngsters. We can discuss each one—their backgrounds and whatever—at your convenience."

Jimmy took the papers and started to say something, when he handed them back to Doctor Peterson. He had heard sounds of a scuffle coming from the bunkhouse. "We'll discuss this later. It sounds like there's something going on already," he said, as he headed toward the bunkhouse.

Inside, he found Holly and Shorty rolling around on the floor, fighting. He immediately put a stop to the fighting. Holding each boy at arm's length, he asked, "What's going on here?"

Neither boy would answer.

"I better get an answer and get one real quick, or I'll treat you like I treat horses that don't get along," said Jimmy.

"How do you treat them?" asked Holly.

"I tie them together so they've only got about six inches between them and turn them loose. They're tied so close they can't fight, so they can't hurt each other and after a time, short or long, they learn to get along. Do you boys want that?"

Both boys shook their heads.

"Then tell me what's going on here," said Jimmy, as he turned both boys loose. "You first Shorty."

"I wanted that bed," said Shorty.

"But I put my stuff on it first," said Holly.

"But I wanted it," countered Shorty.

"What's so special about that bunk?" asked Jimmy.

Silence. Neither boy was willing to admit that this was just a question of dominance between the boys, each one trying to exert superiority over the other.

Mason and Doctor Peterson were standing in the doorway,

watching, while the boys fidgeted nervously. "I would suggest you answer Mister McIntyre. It's not too late to return to town with Mister Mason and if you return to town, it's straight into reform school. There's no more probation if you fail here, this amounts to your last chance."

"Bill and Michael, have you selected your bunks?" asked Jimmy.

"Yes sir!" came the prompt reply.

"Okay then, Shorty and Holly, I will select your bunks for you," said Jimmy. "Shorty, you take this one over here and Holly, you take this one over here. You'll be separated and I suggest you save your strength. You'll need it tomorrow."

"What's going on tomorrow?" asked Michael.

"Just a little surprise," replied Jimmy. "But you'll need your strength. You boys get settled in. Doctor Peterson and I will be just outside. After a bit, we'll take you up and introduce you to the cook then show you around the place."

Mason remained inside as Doctor Peterson and Jimmy left the room and went outside. Once again, Doctor Peterson handed the papers to Jimmy. "These are the boy's files. You can feel free to make any comments in them, good or bad, that you feel appropriate. After a time, the judge and I will review the files to make a final decision as to the future paths we will take with each boy. A brief run down on each boy is warranted, and you can look over their files later."

Doctor Peterson continued, "Shorty appears to have an inferiority complex because of his size and tries to compensate for it by being tough. He may have been a gang leader because he does show some leadership qualities. I hope we can turn those qualities into something worthwhile so he can become a useful member of society.

"Michael appears to be the silent type, although he has quite a long list of minor infractions. You can tell from his record that he really got off on the wrong foot. He appears to be a loner. I suspect he has some alcohol and drug problems.

"Bill has had some drug and alcohol problems. He's been in a rehab house and a halfway house, but keeps going back to his old ways. His drug and alcohol problems have led to his committing crimes to support his bad habits."

"Do either one have any drugs now, prescription or otherwise?" asked Jimmy.

"No," replied the doctor. "They're both clean as a whistle now. Holly is a real question. He may be bi-polar, he may have a split personality, its even been suggested that he's possessed by some sort of demon."

"We all have our demons," replied Jimmy. "What's he doing here? And how old is he?"

"He's fourteen. He does have an extensive criminal record," replied the doctor. "And, as this is an experimental program, the judge thought this might be helpful for him."

"I hope it's helpful to all of them," said Jimmy. "You've got me quite a bunch here—a drug addict alcoholic, a loner, a gang leader, and a schizophrenic. That's quite a mixture to start with."

"But they all have one thing in common," said the doctor. "They're all juvenile delinquents and they all need a fair shot at life, or at least turning their lives around."

"You're right. Let's get the boys and introduce them to Emily. It's about time for dinner?"

"Dinner? You eat early around here."

Jimmy laughed. "Dinner is our noon meal. Supper is your dinner."

At dinner, Emily eyed the new boys suspiciously as she was introduced to them. She did treat them courteously. She remained quiet while the boys ate—and they ate heartily. After dinner Jimmy took the boys out to the corral where the new mustang colts were.

"These are wild horses, young, but still wild," he said. "It will be your job to halter break them and teach them some ground manners. I'll help you, but it will be your job. Have any of you been around horses before?"

"No," was the response.

"I rode one at the fair," said Mike.

"Really?" asked Jimmy.

"Yeah, but it was just in a ring."

"Just going around in a circle attached to a walker?" asked Jimmy.

"Yeah," answered Mike.

"That's not really riding," said Jimmy. "But you will be expected to have these colts as gentle as those ponies."

"Colts? What's a colt?" asked Holly.

"A colt is a young horse," answered Jimmy. "Even though they're young, they can still hurt you. They'll need to learn to trust you and it will be your job to teach them that."

"How do we do that?" asked Shorty.

"That's just one of the things you'll have to learn here. But I can tell you, the horse won't trust you until you trust him," replied Jimmy.

"That sounds backward to me," said Shorty.

"It may sound that way, but that's the way it works," said Jimmy.

Mister Mason approached. "Jimmy, I need to talk to you."

"Sure," said Jimmy. "You boys just stay here and watch the colts. See if you can figure out what they're thinking. Don't go in the corral."

Jimmy and Mason stepped away from the boys. "Do you think it is wise to send Craig off alone with the truck?" Mason was very serious as he asked the question.

"We'll find out," answered Jimmy.

"What if he decides to leave?"

"He won't get far with the state logo on each door. Besides, I told him to take the back road and stay off the highway. He doesn't have a driver's license," said Jimmy.

"No driver's license! Don't you realize you're guilty of contributing to the delinquency of a minor?" Mason sounded quite upset. "We're here trying to rehabilitate these youngsters and you're contributing to their delinquency!"

"Not really," replied Jimmy. Jimmy was relaxed during this conversation. "You don't need a license to drive on private property. If you did, all the farm and ranch kids in the country would be guilty of breaking the law. Most all the country kids can drive by the time they're big enough to reach the pedals."

"But something seems out of place with it," said Mason.

"It's just like I was telling these new kids," said Jimmy. "A horse won't trust you until you trust him. These young kids are pretty much like the colts. We have to trust them before they will trust us. Craig is making good progress and this is a test for him. I expect he'll do well. Emily told him to be back by six for supper. You can stick around and see if he passes the test."

"I'll do just that," said Mason.

"I'll tell Emily to fix extra for supper."

"Don't bother, I already told her."

"Fine," said Jimmy, grinning. "I'll get back to the youngsters and try to help them become acclimated."

The newcomers watched the colts, trying to figure out what they were doing. There were some interesting theories as to what was going on. Some of the colts started to approach the boys out of curiosity.

"Tell me what they're thinking," said Jimmy, as he opened the gate and entered the corral. The colts immediately ran to the far side of the corral and turned to watch Jimmy.

"They're scared of you," said Bill.

"That's right," said Jimmy. "It's our job to eliminate or overcome that fear of humans and replace it with trust."

"How do you that?" asked Holly.

"That's just what we'll learn," replied Jimmy. "It's getting close to suppertime. You guys can go get settled in the bunkhouse and get cleaned up for supper. When you're done with that come up to the kitchen. Emily should just about have supper ready."

Six o'clock came and the boys, Emily, Jimmy, Mason, and Doctor Peterson sat down to eat. Mason appeared to be a little nervous and kept looking at the clock—Craig hadn't showed up yet.

Jimmy noticed this and told Mason, "Relax. Something has come up. Missus Burkhart might have invited him to eat there."

"We can't have something go wrong this early in our program," said Mason. "I'm worried."

"If he's not here by seven, I'll saddle a horse and go look for him," said Jimmy. "We need to give him an even chance."

"I guess you're right," said Mason reluctantly.

After supper was finished, Jimmy assigned each one of the boys a chore to do connected with cleaning up after supper. Bill and Shorty complained about having to wash dishes, but Jimmy stopped the complaints with the comment, "Everyone will have an opportunity to do the dishes. Each one of you has to take your plate to the sink, scrape it and place it by the sink."

Instructions having been given, Jimmy walked down to the barn and caught his horse, Max. He was about to saddle him when he heard a truck approach. It was Craig, but he was almost an hour late.

Jimmy met him in the yard. "You're a little late Craig. Were you having too much fun at the Burkharts?"

Craig smiled at the question. "Hauling hay isn't much fun. I had a flat tire and there wasn't a jack in the truck. I had to walk back to Richard's, ah…, that is, Mister Burkhart's place and borrow a jack. He gave me a ride back to the truck on his four-wheeler and we changed the tire. He said he'd have Missus Burkhart call Emily when he got back and explain that I was going to be a little late."

At that moment, Emily came to the door and called for Jimmy. "Louise is on the phone and said Craig will be a little late. Oh! There he is. I'll tell her he arrived safely. Craig, you come in and eat. I've kept some supper warm for you."

"Go get your supper, Craig," said Jimmy.

"Yes sir," replied Craig as he started toward the house. He noticed Mason and as he passed him said, "Hello Mister Mason."

"Hello Craig," answered Mason.

Mason walked over to where Jimmy was standing. Doctor Peterson joined them.

"Jimmy," said Mason, "I'm impressed. Craig has learned some responsibility and manners in the short time he's been here."

"He'll learn more than that before he leaves, but he is doing better than expected."

"I'm also impressed," said Doctor Peterson. "Just out of curiosity, to what do you attribute the success of this little experiment to?"

"Gentlemen," replied Jimmy, "if you'll pardon my abruptness, you fellows only know these youngsters from their criminal and court records. I've come to know Craig personally, as an individual. I've worked and even played with him. I've watched him in stressful and relaxed situations. I know more about him than you know from his paper records."

"Interesting," said Doctor Peterson. "You have virtually a twenty-four hour a day therapy session with him. I wonder …"

"Only about sixteen hours a day," interrupted Jimmy. "I need my rest time you know!"

The doctor laughed. "You're right. But I wonder if I should spend more time out here observing these youngsters?"

"You could do that," said Jimmy. "But you would need to do more than sit back and observe. You'd need to become involved in what they're doing. You'd need to be out there in the heat, working up a sweat with the youngsters. You'd need to be getting your hands dirty and calloused. You'd need to be doing your share of what the youngsters are doing. We're going over to the Burkharts tomorrow to haul and stack his hay. We'll be leaving here about seven o'clock in the morning. Do you want to go with us?"

"It would be interesting, but I hadn't really planned on staying out here that long. I do have a lot to do at the office. Maybe later at a more convenient date I could arrange it," replied the doctor.

Jimmy smiled at the thought that the doctor, even as big and stout as he was, backed off from the thought of some physical labor. "Well, it was your idea. You can implement it at any time. We've got about three days of hauling Burkhart's hay, then he'll come over here, cut and bale ours and we'll haul it. We're about ten days out from hauling our own hay."

"Ten days, huh?" replied the doctor. "I'll see if I can arrange it."

Jimmy thought the doctor looked a little nervous about arranging his schedule to include some physical work. *He probably won't be able to find the time to come out here and help,* thought Jimmy. *It was a good thought, but probably nothing will come of it.*

But the doctor wasn't nervous about coming out to help. He was thinking about how he could rearrange his schedule so he could come out and help.

Mason and Doctor Peterson made their preparations to leave. "Anything you need from town next time I come out?" asked Mason.

"You might bring out a fairly complete first-aid kit," said Jimmy, thinking about the fight he'd broken up between the boys earlier that day. "And a first-aid book of instructions. You could take that flat tire in and get it fixed."

"Good idea," replied Mason. "You'll have both of them next time I come out."

"Boys," said Jimmy, "it's time to hit the sack. We've got a big day ahead of us tomorrow and you'll need your rest. I'll be getting you up around five-thirty so we can get a good breakfast and an early start. We'll have to do our chores around here before we go. I'd suggest you all hit the sack right away and get a good night's sleep. Don't be sitting up late throwing the bull."

A Little Physical Labor

The next day, Jimmy was up early and walking through the bunk-house hollering, "Up and at 'em, boys! It's time to get up and greet the day! Breakfast is waiting and if it has to wait too long, it'll spoil!"

Slowly the boys got out of bed. It was clear to Jimmy that they weren't used to getting up early. He thought, *Typical of kids today, stay up late at night and sleep in in the morning.*

Craig was already up and dressed, having become somewhat accustomed to getting up earlier in the morning.

"Craig," said Jimmy, "I think I'll make you the bunkhouse boss. It'll be your job to get these guys up every day, make sure they make their beds and clean up the place. I'll tell the boys that at breakfast. Can you do that?"

"I think so," replied Craig.

At breakfast, Jimmy explained to the boys, "Craig is in charge of the bunkhouse and each of you are to do what he tells you to do. If there is a question, you are to do it first, then come to me with any complaints. Any questions?"

The boys were silent.

"Good," said Jimmy. He opened the carton of gloves he'd bought at the horse sale and handed each boy a pair. "You'll need these today. Don't lose them—you only get one pair unless you wear them out."

Craig took his breakfast dishes to the sink, scraped them off, and placed them in the sink.

"Let's see. Bill and Shorty did dishes last night, so it's Holly and

Mike's turn to do dishes this morning. Bill and Shorty can go to the bunkhouse and sweep it out, clean the restroom and generally tidy up the place. Craig and I will do the chores this morning. Emily, you won't have much to do today, other than fix supper, so what do you have planned?"

"I'll put something in the crock pot and go over to the Burkharts and see if I can help Louise fix the noon meal. I'll take some of our groceries. We can't expect them to feed this crew when they're showing up unannounced. I'll take my car."

"That sounds like a plan," said Jimmy. "Let's get started."

When all the chores were done, Jimmy instructed the boys to get in the back of the truck. He and Craig rode in the front. As they drove to the Burkharts, Jimmy asked Craig, "Anything go on in the bunkhouse last night that I should know about?"

"Nothing that I know about," replied Craig. "I think they stayed up pretty late talking. I don't know, I was tired and fell asleep."

"Hopefully, we'll get them tired enough today that they'll hit the sack early and get a good night's rest."

Burkhart smiled when he saw all the extra help arriving with Jimmy. "We can get this done in no time if these other boys are as good as Craig," he said, as the boys climbed out of the truck. It appeared to Jimmy that Burkhart had taken a liking to Craig.

"We'll need to take it easy on them," said Jimmy. "They're fresh out of the city and maybe not in the best physical shape. Emily is bringing some groceries over. She thought she might help Missus Burkhart fix dinner for this crew."

"Good," said Burkhart. "They can fix us a good dinner."

"I also thought you might drive the tractor, seeing as you're still hobbling around on a bum foot," said Jimmy.

"Well, let's get started. With all this extra help, we can get more hay on each load."

"Let me introduce these boys to you," said Jimmy.

"Oh, yes. I forgot my manners."

"This is Bill." As Jimmy said his name, Bill stepped forward and extended his hand to Burkhart. "Bill, this is Mister Burkhart."

Burkhart was surprised. And Jimmy was surprised at Bill's manners. He didn't expect much in manners from these juvenile delinquents. As Jimmy introduced the other boys, Burkhart took the initiative and extended his hand to each one of them. When they had all been introduced, Burkhart said, "Don't get upset if I forget your names. I'm not much good at remembering. Just correct me when I get it wrong."

They got on the wagon and Burkhart drove them to the hay field.

"Boys," said Jimmy, "all we have to do is put these hay bales on this trailer and take them to the ranch and unload them. Mister Burkhart, if you'll drive, I'll show these city boys a little about hauling hay."

"But I ought to be doing the heavy work!" said Burkhart. "It's my hay."

"I really think you ought to drive and give that bum foot a chance to heal," said Jimmy.

"This ain't going to be so bad," said Shorty.

Jimmy and Craig just smiled. "You boys throw the hay on the wagon, Craig and I will stack it."

"You two get to ride?" asked Holly.

"Yep, but you'll all get a chance to stack it," replied Jimmy. "We'll split up the duties as even as we can."

They started loading the hay. At first it was easy. The bales only weighed about seventy pounds or so and the boys had fun seeing who could throw the bales the farthest. Shorty even threw one across the wagon. It landed on the other side and Bill was going to throw it back to Shorty's side of the wagon when Jimmy stopped the horseplay.

"Better stop that," he admonished. "Save your strength. You'll need it when we're stacking the wagon five or six high."

"Five or six high? What do you mean?" asked Bill.

"We're going to put five or six layers of bales on this wagon," answered Jimmy.

"I can throw them that high," said Shorty.

"We'll see," said Jimmy, smiling.

They loaded the wagon to four high and Jimmy had Burkhart stop. He showed the boys how two of them could throw the bales up to the fifth and sixth layer of bales.

"It takes cooperation," he said. "Even though this wagon is built low to the ground, it's still a good distance to throw seventy pounds. And you'll need to do it without pulling the strings off. You'll need to help each other. That's just one of the things you'll learn here."

Jimmy got back on the wagon and they resumed loading the hay. He watched as the boys helped each other throw the bales on. He could see a little cooperation beginning within the crew.

When they had the trailer loaded, the boys climbed on the wagon and sat down.

"I don't want any horseplay riding this load back to the ranch. If one of you fell off, you could be seriously hurt. And if the wagon ran over you, you could even be killed. You need to save your strength because we've got to unload it."

"Then that's it for the day," said Shorty.

"Nope," replied Jimmy. "When it's unloaded, we come back for another load. The way I've got it figured, we'll get three loads this morning and maybe four this afternoon."

"Then we're done?" asked Shorty.

"Nope," replied Jimmy. "We've still got our chores to do back at our place."

"This is beginning to sound like work!" said Shorty.

"It is," said Jimmy, smiling.

From listening to Shorty and watching him work, Jimmy decided that he did have a sense of humor although it was a little sarcastic. He decided Shorty was a smart aleck. It did seem to fit. He figured that because of his shorter size, Shorty needed to be saying something all the time, just to make sure everyone knew he was there.

Burkhart had a portable gasoline elevator to get the bales up to the hayloft. Burkhart, Craig, Bill, and Shorty were on top of the elevator stacking the hay and Jimmy, Holly, and Mike kept the elevator loaded. They could only put three bales at a time on the elevator and this gave Burkhart time to instruct the boys on how he wanted the hay stacked.

They unloaded the hay and went back for another load. They got three loads and left the last one to unload after dinner.

"What's for lunch?" asked Shorty, as they all entered the house.

"It's not lunch," said Emily. "It's dinner."

"You mean we have to work as hard as we did and only get one meal for it?" asked Shorty.

Emily, Louise, and Jimmy laughed. Even Richard Burkhart smiled.

"No," replied Emily. "Out here the noon meal is dinner and the evening meal is supper."

"You people have some weird ways," commented Shorty. "What do we get to eat?"

"Sloppy Joes," answered Louise. "And there's plenty!"

The boys ate heartedly, as did Burkhart and Jimmy.

"Are you ready to get back to work?" asked Jimmy.

The boys nodded that they were, but they didn't look like they wanted to.

"I think we better set some and let dinner settle," said Burkhart. "As much as they ate, they've got more to carry around now. Rest a spell, boys, and tell me about yourselves, we've hauled more hay this morning than I thought we would. You start, Shorty, I think you've got plenty to say."

Jimmy looked at Burkhart with surprise. The older man wasn't the mean, grouchy man he started out to be. He was really quite considerate and compassionate.

Shorty gave a brief history of himself, careful not to mention anything about his problems with the law. Each of the other boys followed, not mentioning anything about their law problems.

Jimmy noticed this and so did Burkhart. When they got done, Burkhart said, "I understand you are all here because you've had some run-ins with law enforcement. Well, I don't care about that. If you work on the rehabilitation ranch as hard as you've worked this morning, you should get along okay."

"You mean this isn't a dude ranch and we're not here for our summer vacation?" exclaimed Shorty.

Everyone laughed, even Burkhart.

Jimmy noticed this and also noticed what he perceived to be a change in Burkhart's attitude. He thought, *Perhaps this might be a rehabilitation project for everyone. Burkhart seems to be more at ease around these youngsters than the first time Craig and I met him.*

Emily, after helping Louise with the dishes, came out on the porch and announced, "I'll be going back to our place and start supper. What time will you be back?"

"Better figure around six, maybe a little later, depending on how much we can get done this afternoon," answered Jimmy.

"Supper will be ready whenever you show up," said Emily.

Playing With the Colts

The hay hauling went on for another four days. It was hard work and the boys were tired and showed it. Everyone took their rightful turns at throwing hay on the wagon or stacking it. After the first day, there wasn't any one sitting up late talking. The boys were ready to go to bed after supper.

Emily showed up every day to help Louise fix the noon meal.

The evening of the last day hauling Burkhart's hay, Burkhart said, "We've hauled all this in faster than the Missus and I did. I figure we're a day and a half faster, maybe two days faster than before. I surely want to thank you all for helping me out. I'll be over in the morning to start cutting your hay."

"You mean we have to do this again?" asked Shorty.

"Only if you want to feed your livestock during the winter," replied Burkhart.

"But we've been feeding our horses every morning and night!" said Shorty.

"Yep," said Jimmy. "And you've eaten every morning and night too! You've also got a noon meal, those horses didn't."

Shorty didn't say anything, except, "I thought we were done."

"Ranch work is never done," said Jimmy. "But tomorrow, we get to do something different. It won't be as strenuous as hauling hay, but there is an element of danger. You could get hurt."

"What is it?" asked Bill.

"Tomorrow, we'll start halter-breaking the colts."

"How can that be dangerous?" asked Holly. "They don't look so mean to me."

"They aren't naturally mean," replied Jimmy. "But they've never been around people before and won't know what to expect. They'll probably expect the worst."

Mike asked, "We aren't going to hurt them, are we?"

"We might hurt them a little to start, but hopefully they'll get over it fast. They're young yet, so they should learn pretty fast. Once they learn something, we'll have to keep doing it, they forget pretty fast at their young ages."

"How are we going to do it?" asked Shorty.

"I'll show you in the morning."

The next morning, after breakfast and the morning chores were done, and Burkhart had showed up and started cutting hay, Jimmy gathered the youngsters. "Craig, would you go to the barn and bring out the colt halters we bought at the sale? And don't forget the long lead ropes."

Craig went to the barn and returned with the halters and lead ropes.

"We're going to start halter-breaking these colts today," said Jimmy. "Be careful and don't get kicked. I'll rope one and show you how to do it. They'll learn pretty fast at this age."

Jimmy got his lariat from his saddle and roped a colt. The boys were surprised at the fight the colt put up at the end of the rope. Jimmy held on and when the colt had pretty well choked himself down and threw himself to the ground, he took a halter and put it on the colt. Then he loosened the lariat around the colt's neck and, holding the lead rope, let the colt up.

"This is where you have to be especially careful," he said, as the colt got up. "Not only can you get kicked by his hind feet, but he can strike you with his front feet. And you need to keep hold of the lead rope. He'll try to get away from you, but hold on!"

The colt got up and immediately tried to get away. Jimmy kept him under control, careful not to get kicked or struck by the colt's feet. He let the colt get close to the fence then quickly tied him to a fence post.

"Now, we'll let him stand there until he figures out that he can't fight the rope. He'll teach himself how to be tied. I'll rope another one. Which one of you boys wants to halter him?"

Nobody said anything. Finally, Shorty said, "I'll try."

"Okay," said Jimmy. "You'll need to be quick, we don't want to choke him to death."

Jimmy roped a colt and choked him down. When the colt threw himself, Jimmy hollered, "Get up to him and get that halter on him, quick!"

Shorty started toward the colt and Jimmy hollered again, "Stay away from his feet! He can still kick you while he's lying on the ground!"

Shorty changed his approach, and after some struggling, finally got the halter on the colt.

"Now take off the lariat rope and let him up!" hollered Jimmy. "And hold on! Let him work himself toward the fence and tie him to a post."

"I don't know how to tie!" hollered Shorty.

It occurred to Jimmy that he hadn't shown the boys the knot he used to tie the colt to the fence.

"Hold on, I'll come help you."

With that, Jimmy took the lead rope, maneuvered the colt to the fence, and tied him up.

"That wasn't too bad," he said when the colt was tied up. "Now I'll show you how to tie a slip knot that you can always get undone. Mike, you hold this end. This is the end the colt is hooked to. Now watch. Take this piece, make a loop, and lay this piece in the loop and take this end through the loop, making sure you have the tail coming here. You can always get it undone by pulling the tail. Depending on how hard the colt pulls against it and tightens it, you might have to pull it pretty hard. Now each one of you boys try it and keep trying it until you have it down pat. Take turns. When you think you've got it, let me know and I'll give it the test."

"The test? What's that?" asked Bill.

"The test is simple," said Jimmy. "I pull the tail of the rope. If it comes loose, it's tied right. If it doesn't, it's not. You boys work on it for a while. We've got plenty of time, we've only got six more to catch."

About that time a car pulled into the yard and Jimmy went to see who was visiting and what they wanted. He thought he recognized the driver, but wasn't sure. As the driver approached him, Jimmy felt like he'd known him, but couldn't put a name on him.

As the driver approached Jimmy, he extended his hand and said, "Dale Williams. I met you over at the Wilson Ranch and met you again a few weeks ago."

"Oh, yes," replied Jimmy. "I remember. What can I do for you?"

"I was talking with Bill Mason and he said you might be able to use some help out here. He sent this," he said, as he reached in his pocket and pulled out an envelope.

Jimmy took the envelope, opened it up and read it.

"It says here that Mason has given his approval for you to volunteer out here," said Jimmy.

"That's right," replied Dale.

"You can volunteer, but we're not in a position to offer any money for your services," said Jimmy. "Aren't you one of Mason's former, ah … clients?"

"Right again," said Dale.

"What do you think you can do out here and why do you want to volunteer?"

"Mason treated me pretty nice and helped me out quite a bit. I'd kinda like to repay him. When I told him what I wanted, he suggested this. It was his idea."

"How long do you figure on staying?"

"Until you don't need me anymore," replied Dale.

"I guess we can put you to work, but I don't know where we'll put you up. We can't have you staying with the boys."

"Put him in your room on the cot Craig was using before he

25

moved into the bunkhouse." It was Emily. She'd approached when she saw Dale's car arrive. "You need to send a boy out to get Richard for dinner. It's that time."

"I'll send Craig," said Jimmy. "I'll show you where to put your stuff. Bring in Dale's stuff, boys," he yelled, "its dinnertime. Come to the house. Craig, would you go get Mister Burkhart and bring him to dinner?"

"Yes sir!" replied Craig.

At dinner, everyone was introduced to Dale Williams. "He'll be helping out here for a while," said Jimmy.

"I thought he looked too old to be a juvenile delinquent," said Shorty, laughing.

Jimmy shot a look to Shorty that implied, "That'll be enough of that."

Dale just smiled. He'd been a juvenile delinquent in his younger years. He was just volunteering here as a sort of payback for what the Wilson's and Bill Mason had done for him.

After dinner, Jimmy and the boys went back to halter-breaking the colts. Before they started, Jimmy made sure they all had mastered the slip knot he had taught them.

"What do you want me to do?" asked Dale.

"Just kinda watch and help make sure the kids don't get hurt. But don't be doing it for them. This is their job."

Each one of the colts was caught and tied to a corral post. "We'll just let them stand for a while. They'll soon figure out that they can't fight the lead rope. We'll keep an eye on them and be ready to help them if they get themselves in trouble."

"How can they get in trouble?" asked Bill.

"They might get a leg over the lead rope," said Jimmy. "Or they might throw themselves and be hanging. They'll need help if they do that. By the way, the lead rope should only have about an arm's length from the colt to the corral post. There's one over there that's a little long. Watch as I walk up to the colt and shorten it."

Jimmy walked up to the colt slowly, speaking softly as he went.

He reached out to pet the colt and the colt reared back. When he came down he had a leg over the rope.

Jimmy quickly pulled the slip knot loose, but kept a hold on the rope. He was trying to pet the colt, but he kept backing away from him. Jimmy kept a hold of the lead rope and finally, when the colt had backed up into a corner of the corral, Jimmy got a hold of the lead rope close to the halter and got the rope from between the colt's legs.

Continuing to talk softly to the colt, Jimmy reached out and patted the colt on the forehead. "Do you like that, little guy?" he asked. "We'll just keep it up a little longer."

Without raising his voice, he asked the boys, "Did you see that? Without spooking this little guy, come over here slowly and talk softly to the colt."

The colt spooked when Mike jumped down off the fence.

"Easy," admonished Jimmy. "This guy is already scared, we don't want to scare him more. Just take your time coming over here."

"Sorry," said Mike.

The colt tried to get away as the boys approached, but Jimmy kept a good hold on him.

"What did you boys notice when I came up to this colt?" he asked.

"The colt wanted to get away," said Bill.

"That's right," said Jimmy. "But he couldn't, could he? Why did he want to get away?"

"He didn't know you were going to help him," said Mike.

"That's partially correct," replied Jimmy. "What else?"

"Fear," volunteered Shorty.

"Right! We have to overcome his natural fear of humans. Any ideas on how we're going to do this, Holly?"

"Nope," answered Holly.

"Anybody got any ideas?" asked Jimmy.

There was silence.

"How about familiarity?" Jimmy asked.

"Familiarity? What does that have to do with it?" asked Bill.

"Everything," replied Jimmy. "You don't trust anybody you don't know, do you? You probably don't trust everyone you do know. We want to teach these colts that we're not going to harm them, we want to be their friends. We want them to trust us."

"How do we teach that?" asked Mike. "I've never had a horse for a friend before. I do know a couple of jackasses!"

Everyone laughed at Mike's comment, even Jimmy.

"A horse can be a good friend and we all know a few jackasses," said Jimmy, still laughing. "The way we teach that is by doing everything the same way every time. We work into it slowly. A lot of petting, soft words, and gentle action. We reward good behavior and punish bad behavior. Just like people. In fact, we can learn a lot about people from horses. These colts will learn to trust us fairly quickly. But remember, a horse won't trust us completely until we trust him.

"What else did you see as I got close to the colt?"

Again there was silence.

"As I walked up to the colt," said Jimmy, "I was talking to him softly. It didn't make any difference what I was saying, I could have been reciting the Declaration of Independence, the colt doesn't understand. The fact is that I was talking to him as soothingly as I could. Always remember this: each time you approach a horse, talk to him. And talk easy. It always helps. And it lets the horse know where you are. Any questions?"

There weren't any questions from the boys.

"Okay," said Jimmy. "Now, each one of you boys, using what you just learned, go get a colt and see if you can pet him. Don't get kicked! I'll be watching."

Jimmy went to the far side of the corral to watch. He took Dale with him.

"We'll be lucky if none of these kids gets hurt," said Dale.

"Yep," replied Jimmy. "But it comes with the territory. Be ready to help someone if he needs it, but don't be too anxious."

Jimmy and Dale watched as the boys approached the colts.

Shorty actually made it up to one colt and patted him on the head before anyone else. Mike started to approach a colt, but when the colt pulled back then jumped forward, Mike ran away.

Dale laughed and Jimmy just smiled and said, "Give it another shot! He doesn't know what to expect. Go slower."

Hearing Jimmy's advice to Mike, Bill and Holly took more time and actually were petting their colts by the time Mike got to his colt. Craig had gotten to a colt shortly after Shorty and was making good progress with him.

"Now," said Jimmy, "just pet them for a while. Familiarity, that's what we're trying to get. Pet them all over, as far as you can. Remember, no sudden movements. We'll do this for half an hour or so, then start on the others."

In due time, the boys left the colts they'd began with and started on the others. They had about the same result, although a colt reared and knocked Shorty down. He wasn't hurt—more embarrassed than anything. He wasn't used to being laughed at.

Dale went over to help him up.

"I'm all right," said Shorty.

"A little over-confidant, perhaps?" volunteered Dale.

There was no answer from Shorty, but he went right back to approaching the colt.

When all the colts had been approached and petted for about half an hour, Jimmy said, "We'll call it a day now. Turn the colts loose, but leave the halters and lead ropes on them, they'll be easier to catch tomorrow. And they'll learn to give in to the ropes. We'll do the feeding and take the rest of the day off."

The next day, after breakfast and the morning chores were done, the colts were caught up again and tied to the corral. They were easier to catch with the halters and lead ropes on. They were allowed to stand tied for a time. For the most part, they were easier to approach, although Holly got kicked in the leg. He let out a howl and tried to kick the colt back in retaliation, but he missed. He was trying again when Jimmy hollered,

"Hold on! That's not how we teach trust."

"But he kicked me and I was trying to punish him," said Holly.

"You don't want to get into a kicking match with a horse," said Jimmy. "Remember, a horse has four legs to stand on. When he's kicking you, depending on how he's doing it, he still has two or three legs to stand on. When you're kicking him, you only have one leg to stand on. You're at an immediate disadvantage."

"But how do you punish him?" asked Holly.

"We're not looking so much to punish him for bad behavior as we're looking to reward him for good behavior," said Jimmy. "A sharp tug on the lead rope will tell him that he's done wrong. Then we'll end on a good note. Just keep petting him, he'll settle down."

After each colt had been caught, tied, and successfully approached and petted, they were allowed to stand tied to the corral.

"Now, we're going to teach the colts how to lead, how to follow us around where we want to go," said Jimmy. "This will take cooperation between you boys and the colts. Dale and I will show you how to do it, then you boys will pair up and do it. Dale, pick a colt and we'll get started. I'll be right back."

Jimmy went to the truck and brought out a livestock prod, about six feet long, and returned.

"That's what I needed when that little bugger kicked me," said Holly.

"We're not going to use this for punishment," said Jimmy. "When Dale gives a tug on the lead rope, I'll use this prod and touch the colt on the rump. He'll probably jump forward, so Dale has to be watching so he doesn't get run over. Watch. Dale, are you ready?'

"I'm ready, Jimmy."

"Let's get started."

Jimmy watched Dale and when Dale gave the lead rope a tug, he used the prod to touch the colt on the rump. At the touch on the rump, the colt jumped forward, almost running over Dale. Dale stepped aside and the colt ran past him, but Dale kept a hold on the lead rope.

Dale pulled the lead rope and the colt turned around and faced him, with a look on his face that seemed to ask, "Is that what you wanted?"

Dale got closer to the colt's head and petted him between the ears. He gave the lead rope another tug. The colt took a step forward and Dale again petted him between the ears, saying, "That's a good little horse."

"That's good," said Jimmy, as he walked around behind the colt. "We just do this one step at a time. Let him stand for a bit, then give him another tug."

Dale did as he was told and the colt took another step forward. The process was repeated and soon the colt was following Dale readily.

"The fact that I'm behind the colt is helping him to move forward," said Jimmy. "He can see me and he doesn't want to get poked on the rump with this prod, so he's yielding to the pull on the lead rope. He'll soon figure out that a tug on the lead means move forward, and I won't have to follow him.

"Now, you boys pair up and each pair can start a colt. We'll have to do it one pair at a time, we only have one prod. While one pair of boys is working a colt, the rest of you can watch and see what the boys teaching are doing right or wrong."

The boys paired up with Shorty and Bill going first.

"I'll use the stick," said Shorty.

Bill got a colt and Shorty poked the colt in the rump. The colt jumped forward, knocking Bill down. He lost the lead rope.

"Are you okay?" asked Jimmy, as he went to help Bill up.

"Yeah," answered Bill as he got up and brushed the dust off.

"Catch that colt and try it again," said Jimmy. "Shorty, you just give the colt a gentle tap on the rump with the prod. Don't jab him! Remember, you and Bill are going to change positions on another colt."

Bill caught the colt and they resumed the lesson. This time Shorty was not so aggressive with the prod.

Jimmy returned to where he and Dale had been watching.

"Do you think Shorty was doing that intentionally?" asked Dale.

"Very possibly," replied Jimmy. "Shorty does seem to have an aggressive nature about him. It seems like he's always trying to assert himself. He might need watching."

Bill and Shorty soon had the colt leading, repeating the procedure Jimmy and Dale had been using.

Holly and Mike started another colt. By noon, they had half the colts leading. Emily came down to the corral and announced, "It's dinner time! Craig, would you go get Richard?"

"Boys, go get cleaned up," said Jimmy.

The boys went to the bunkhouse and washed. When they returned, Burkhart was washing up in the kitchen sink. He was telling Jimmy, "I should be done sometime this afternoon or tomorrow. We'll let the hay cure for a couple of days, then I'll be over to bale it. I'll be over early, we'll try to bale as much as we can with the dew on it to keep the leaves. What have you boys been doing?"

"We're teaching the colts," replied Shorty.

"Teaching them what?" asked Burkhart.

"We're teaching them reward and punishment," said Shorty.

Jimmy noticed Shorty's reply and noted his emphasis on the word punishment. He thought, *He missed the fact that the boys are also learning cooperation among themselves and the colts.*

"We'll finish with the rest of the colts this afternoon, then tomorrow I'll take each one of you for a horseback ride," said Jimmy. "While some of us are out riding, the others can continue to teach the colts."

"What else do we have to teach them?" asked Holly.

"They need to be brushed from head to tail, under their bellies, down to their feet. They need to have their feet picked up. We need to teach them all the things they'll need to know to have good ground manners when they grow up. It'll be pretty easy, they'll learn to like the brushing if we do it right. Picking up their feet might be a little difficult, but we'll teach them that."

"Why do we need to pick up their feet?" asked Mike.

"They need to learn how to be shod. If we do a good job of that now, they'll be easy to shoe when they've grown up. We want to teach them everything they need to know as adult horses now, then when they're big enough to ride, a guy can just get on and ride off. Hopefully, there won't be any buck in them. We'll even saddle them with that small kid's saddle in the barn. There's still plenty to do.

"And," continued Jimmy, "We need to work each one of the colts every day, even after we're done hauling hay."

"We still have to haul hay?" asked Mike

"Yep. That hay won't come here on its own. We've got some hard work and long days ahead of us."

A Little Respite

The afternoon went pretty much like the morning. Shorty almost got run over when Bill jabbed his colt a little too hard. Jimmy noticed this and thought to himself, *He's trying to get even.*

When two other boys were working a colt, Jimmy took Shorty and Bill off to the side to have a little discussion with them.

"It looks like to me," he said, "that there's a little animosity between you two. I don't want to go into details, but you two need to get over it now. You'll be doing things together as long as you're here. I have a friend that had two horses that didn't get along. So he tied them together so that there was only about six inches apart at the heads. After a time, the horses settled their differences. I can't tie you two together, but I can make sure you're both teamed up every chance I get. You better settle your differences now and learn to get along."

Jimmy was very firm and strong in his tone of voice and both boys responded with a hearty, "Yes sir!"

The next day, Jimmy got the boys lined out leading the colts and brushing them. Then he saddled and bridled his horse, Digger, saddled and bridled Max and saddled and bridled the new horse he'd bought at the sale barn. He hadn't settled on a name for the new horse and decided he'd let the boys name him.

"I suppose I ought to take Shorty and Bill out together first," he told the new horse as he bridled him. "We'll let one of them name you. But I think I'll have a little fun first. I'll call you Killer, just to see what the boys' reactions are."

He led Digger out to the corral and tied him to the fence, then went back and got Max and the new horse.

"Shorty and Bill, come over here. Have either one of you ridden before?"

"Nope," answered both boys.

"Then come over into this other pen and I'll give you a short riding lesson," said Jimmy. "You'll ride these horses."

"What are their names?" asked Bill.

"This one is Max. I haven't named the other one, but I've been calling him Killer. Who wants which horse?"

"I'll take Max," said Bill, hurriedly.

"Then I get Killer," said Shorty, apprehensively.

"I haven't named him yet," said Jimmy. "We'll get around to that later. Bill, you get on and I'll adjust your stirrups."

"How do you do that?"

It was obvious to Jimmy that he had some real greenhorns.

"Put your left foot in this stirrup, take a hold of the saddle horn and spring up into the seat." As he said this, he demonstrated. "Now you do it," he said as he got off.

He gave the reins to Bill and said, "Hold on to these loosely. They're what you use to control the horse. They're called reins."

Bill took the reins and immediately pulled back on them. Max started to back up.

"Loosely," said Jimmy, "loosely! When you pull back, you're telling the horse to back up."

Bill gave the reins some slack and Max stopped backing up.

"Now, get on."

Bill put his foot in the stirrup and pulled himself into the saddle.

"Just sit there and we'll get Shorty into the saddle," said Jimmy as he adjusted the stirrups. "Don't pull back or Max will back up."

When he had both stirrups adjusted, he said, "Now stand up. I like an inch or two between me and the saddle. How does that feel."

"Fine, I guess," answered Bill.

"Now you get on, Shorty."

Shorty got on as he'd seen Jimmy and Bill do it. Jimmy adjusted his stirrups then got on his own horse.

"We'll give you a short riding lesson then go."

Jimmy demonstrated how to get the horse to move and said, "Give the reins some slack and touch the horse in the belly with your heels at the same time. To get him to stop, pull back on the reins. When he stops, give him some slack. To get him to turn left, move your hand to the left, laying the reins on the right side of his neck and touch your right heel to the right side of his belly. To go right, just do the opposite. Got it?"

The boys nodded.

"Good. Now you do it."

The boys started their horses. Shorty kicked his horse rather than just touching him and the horse jumped forward. Shorty almost fell off, but he had a tight hold on the saddle horn.

"Just touch him with your heels," advised Jimmy. "Don't kick him! He'll respond differently to a kick than to a touch. That's it. Now turn him left and right. Now stop him. Any questions? If not, we'll go. Follow me."

Jimmy opened the gate from horseback and they started out. As they left, they passed the corral where the other boys were brushing the colts.

"Keep an eye on things here, Dale. We'll be back in about an hour."

They rode out to where Burkhart was cutting the hay.

"What's that smell?" asked Shorty, as they approached the hay field.

"That's the smell of new mown hay," replied Jimmy. "It's real nice, isn't it?"

"Yes," replied Shorty.

"You don't smell anything like it in town, unless somebody's cutting the lawn or a golf course."

They met Burkhart. He stopped the swather to visit a spell. "I thought I might have got done yesterday, but the hay is a little thicker than I thought. I can't go as fast," he said.

"That's good," said Jimmy. "There'll be plenty."

"How are the boys doing?" asked Burkhart.

"They're doing good," answered Jimmy. "They've been teaching the colts a lot and they might have even learned a little themselves."

"What have the boys learned?" asked Burkhart, gruffly.

"Maybe how to get along with the colts and each other," replied Jimmy.

"I guess that's good," said Burkhart. "Everyone needs to learn to get along with each other."

Jimmy thought this last remark from Burkhart was kinda strange. He seemed to be rather gruff and rough around other people.

They visited a little bit then Jimmy said, "We've got to get going. We've got two other boys to get horseback this afternoon. It's getting close to dinnertime, don't be late."

"Sure," said Burkhart as he started the swather.

Jimmy and the boys started back toward the ranch. It was about dinnertime when they got there. Jimmy sent the boys to get cleaned up, unbridled the horses and turned them loose in the corral where they could get something to eat and drink.

When he went to the kitchen, Dale, Burkhart, and the boys were seated at the table, eating.

"How did your ride go?" asked Emily.

"Fine," replied Jimmy. "Anything unusual happen here?"

"Nope," replied Dale.

"Fine," said Jimmy. "I'll take Holly and Mike out this afternoon, then we'll let Craig give Dale a tour of the ranch."

"I'd like to go with you this afternoon," said Emily. "It's been a while since I've been horseback, and I'm beginning to feel a little cramped in this kitchen."

"You can certainly come with us anytime," said Jimmy. "We do need to keep the cook happy. Dale, can you supervise Shorty and Bill? They can spend more time leading the colts and brushing them. The more the colts are worked with, the better off they are."

After dinner, Emily saddled her horse while Jimmy got Holly and Mike on their horses and their stirrups adjusted. When Emily arrived at the corral, Jimmy had her give the boys a brief lesson on how to handle their horses. It was about the same as Jimmy's instructions to Shorty and Mike earlier in the day, other than Emily neglecting to instruct the boys on how to use their heels as leg cues when turning the horse. Jimmy added this and they rode out.

They went to the same places where Jimmy had gone earlier, but they didn't stop to visit with Burkhart. He was almost done cutting hay.

When they got back to the corrals, Emily went straight to the barn, unsaddled her horse, and went to the kitchen to fix supper. Jimmy went to the corrals and gave Holly and Mike's horses to Craig and Dale.

"Give Dale the high dollar tour of the ranch," Jimmy told Craig. "But don't be late for supper. We'll be waiting for you."

Jimmy adjusted Dale's stirrups and then went to the barn and unsaddled Digger. When he returned to the corral, he found Shorty and Bill rolling on the ground. Holly and Mike were watching, not making any effort to break up the fight.

"What's going on here?" Jimmy demanded.

"I wanted to brush this colt and Shorty wouldn't let me," said Bill.

"That's easily fixed," said Jimmy. "Shorty, you brush this side and Bill, you brush the other."

"What good will that do?" asked Shorty.

"For one thing, it will help teach you boys to get along together. Second, we have to teach a horse the same thing on each side. What you teach on the near side, you have to teach on the off side. The horse can't differentiate that what's good on one side will be good on the other. "

"Near side and off side. What's that?" asked Bill.

"The near side is the horse's left side and the off side is his right side," answered Jimmy. "You boys brush each one of these horses that way until you've brushed them all. It will do the colts some good and it might even help you."

Shorty gave Jimmy a disgusted look and went to brushing the off side of the colt.

"You can brush the near side, Bill. I'll be keeping an eye on both of you. Holly, you and Mike can do the same thing."

All the boys were still brushing the colts when Craig and Dale returned. They unsaddled their horses and walked to the corral.

"You've got a pretty nice little place here, Jimmy," said Dale.

"It does have some possibilities," replied Jimmy. "You know, almost everything here was donated, from the land to the bunkhouse to these colts. We even have some cows up on the mountain that came with the ranch. Let's do the evening chores and get ready for supper."

"Sounds good to me," said Dale.

On the way to supper, Jimmy asked, "How do you boys like horseback riding?"

"It's okay," answered Bill.

"It's fun," replied Holly and Mike.

Shorty didn't say anything. That was a little out of character for him.

"What do you think, Shorty?"

"I'm not sure yet," said Shorty. "But I do know that I've got some muscles I didn't know I had!"

Everyone laughed.

"You'll get used to that," said Jimmy.

At supper, Dale asked, "You need a few more horses, don't you?"

"Yes," replied Jimmy.

"How are you going to get them?"

"I really don't know," answered Jimmy. "But we'll need them if all these boys are going to help gather cows this fall. We're short three horses, four if you'll be around then."

"I expect to be around then. I have an idea," said Dale, "but I'll have to be gone a couple of days."

"You don't plan on being gone while we're hauling hay, do you?" Jimmy asked the question with a grin on his face.

"I was hoping to avoid that," said Dale, detecting the humor in Jimmy's question. "But I don't think I can."

"We certainly hope not!" chuckled Jimmy. "What's your plan?"

"I can't say until I see if it will work," said Dale. "If it works, you'll have enough horses."

A Totally Unexpected Surprise

The next few days were spent brushing the colts and leading them around. The boys even had a few trotting after them as they ran. Jimmy was pleased with the progress the colts were making. They had gentled down real nicely. As far as he could tell, there was no animosity among the boys. They appeared to be getting along with each other.

One morning while the boys were working the colts, Emily came down to the corral. "Richard called. He said he'd be over in the morning to start hauling hay. He's bringing his portable elevator and he'll be here early."

"How early?" queried Jimmy.

"About sunup, he said."

"We'll need breakfast early then. We don't want to keep him waiting," said Jimmy. "We'll all need to hit the sack early."

After supper, Jimmy advised everyone to hit the sack early. "We get to haul hay again!"

There were some groans of dismay from the boys.

Noting the dismay, Jimmy said, "Don't worry. There's not as much as there was over at Mister Burkhart's. We should have it stacked in two or three days. We'll be starting earlier and we've got to do our chores before we go. So be ready!"

The next morning, Jimmy was up earlier and got the boys to breakfast. They were just finishing the chores when Burkhart showed up with the tractor and trailer.

"Ready?" he questioned.

"Ready as we'll ever be," answered Jimmy.

"Get on the trailer boys," said Burkhart. "We're going."

When they got to the hayfield, Jimmy said, "Mister Burkhart, you drive. Craig and I will stack and the boys can throw the hay. Boys, we'll take turns throwing the hay, just like we did before. Let's go!"

The morning was spent hauling hay. The first load went over to the Burkhart's. The boys enjoyed the ride to the Burkhart ranch. They had a chance to ride and rest rather than walk and work. They used the elevator to stack the hay on top of the hay that had already been stacked.

"I think we'll put the rest of the hay at your place," said Burkhart.

"But we haven't got your half yet!" said Jimmy.

"I think we have," said Burkhart. "You've provided a lot more help than I ever had before. We'll call that even."

Seeing that he had a good deal coming, Jimmy didn't argue.

By mid-morning they had started to stack hay at the Rehabilitation Ranch. Emily came down to the stack yard with a pitcher of lemonade and a handful of paper cups.

"You boys look like you need a break. Here," she said, handing out the cups.

"You must have been sent from heaven," said Dale.

"I'll second that," said Shorty.

They all sat down and took a break as they drank the lemonade. After the break, Dale found it difficult to get back to work.

"I'm not in as good a shape as I thought I was," said Dale.

"You'll be in good shape just about the time we get done," laughed Jimmy.

About five o'clock, when they'd finished unloading hay, Burkhart said, "We'll call it a day. I've still got my chores to do."

"Good," said Jimmy. "We've got our chores to do, too! And we still have to play with the colts. We don't want them forgetting what we've taught them!"

"I'll be here early again tomorrow," said Burkhart.

"We'll be ready," said Jimmy.

During supper, Dale announced that he'd be leaving in the morning to try and put his plan into action.

"You sure you're not trying to get out of work?" asked Jimmy, with a grin on his face.

"Certainly not!" replied Dale indigently. "But you'll be thanking me if I can do what I've got planned."

After supper that night, a truck and camper showed up in the yard. Jimmy saw the lights as the truck approached and wondered, *Who can that be this time of night?* He went out to greet the visitor.

It was Doctor Peterson, the psychologist.

"What are you doing here this time of night?" asked Jimmy.

"I thought it might be about time to evaluate these boys."

"You mean you didn't come to help haul hay?" asked Jimmy.

The doctor replied, "No, no. Is that what you're doing now?"

"Yep. And you're just in time to help!"

"But I didn't bring any work clothes! I came to do our first evaluation. Let's take a look at the boys' files."

Jimmy took the doctor into the kitchen.

"Have you had your supper yet? We might get Emily to fix you some leftovers."

"I've already eaten," said the Doctor. "I'd like to see the files."

"I'll get them," said Jimmy, as he left the room. Soon he returned with the boys' files and set them on the table in front of the doctor.

The doctor looked over each file carefully. "You've made some good notes here," he said. "But most of it is positive. I really expected to see more negative entries."

"We've kept these boys pretty busy. There hasn't been much time for them to get into trouble. We've tried to keep everything positive here. The only real negative entry is in Shorty and Bill's files. They gotten into a little scuffle, a little disagreement, but I think we've solved the problem."

"How?"

Jimmy explained how two horses that didn't get along were

43

necked together until they worked out their problem. He ended by saying, "I've had those two boys doing everything they had to do, together. So far, it seems to be working."

"Interesting," said the doctor. "I'd like to spend a little time talking to each one of the boys tomorrow. Will that be possible?"

"Why sure, if you're willing to come to the hayfield. You going to stay in the camper tonight?"

"I thought I would," answered the doctor. "But I wanted to talk to the boys privately."

"Well, you just follow us out to the hayfield," said Jimmy. "We'll give each boy time to talk to you in your truck. Then when you're done, you can come help in the hay."

"That'll be fine, but I didn't bring any work clothes or gloves. What time are you getting up?"

"Before sunrise, and I can lend you an old pair of pants and gloves," answered Jimmy.

The doctor looked disappointed.

Noticing this, Jimmy said, "Don't worry. I'll come and rap on your door. You'll be up in time for breakfast."

The next morning, Jimmy rapped on Doctor Peterson's camper and hollered, "Time to get up!" He opened the door and tossed in an old pair of pants and a pair of gloves.

"What time is it?" asked the doctor groggily as he rolled out of bed.

"It's a little after four-thirty. Get up! Times a wasting!"

"The sun isn't even up yet!" moaned the doctor.

"We're not waiting on the sun!" said Jimmy. "Breakfast is ready. Hurry or you'll miss it!"

Jimmy then went to the bunkhouse to wake up the boys. Much to his surprise, he found the boys all up and getting dressed.

"I'm impressed," said Jimmy. "What's got into all of you?"

"Craig told us that the quicker we got started, the quicker we'd be done. Hauling hay isn't much fun," said Shorty.

Jimmy gave Craig an approving look, and said, "Emily has breakfast ready."

Jimmy accompanied the boys to the kitchen and found Dale and Doctor Peterson already eating. Jimmy noted that the doctor didn't have on the old pair of pants that he'd tossed into the camper. Apparently, the doctor wasn't planning on helping in the hay.

After breakfast the boys started the morning chores. They were just about done when Burkhart showed up with the tractor and trailer.

"Ready to go boys? Get on and we'll get started!"

Before Jimmy got on the trailer, he told the doctor, "Follow the tractor out to the hayfield. Just park by the gate." Then he asked, "You're not planning on helping out?"

"No. I've got too much to do back at the office and I'll have to analyze the information I get from the boys."

Jimmy didn't say anything, but thought, *That's part of the problem today. Too much analyzing.*

When they got to the hayfield, Jimmy took Shorty to Doctor Peterson. "When you're done, send him out and I'll send another boy to you."

They started loading and when they had the trailer loaded, Doctor Peterson had only talked to two of the boys.

When Burkhart drove the tractor past the doctor's pickup and camper, Jimmy told him, "We'll need everyone to unload and stack. You can continue when we come back to the field."

They took the hay to the stack yard and unloaded it. Shorty and Holly had already visited with the doctor and when they all returned to the hayfield, Jimmy had Bill visit with him. The rest of them returned to loading the hay.

Jimmy noticed that Bill seemed to be spending more time than the others with his visit. When Bill was done, he returned to the trailer and Jimmy sent Mike over for his visit. When Mike was done the doctor accompanied him to the trailer.

"Jimmy, can I talk to you for a bit before I go?" he asked.

"Sure. Can you boys load the rest of this?"

The boys on the trailer nodded affirmatively.

"The boys seem to be improving," said the doctor. "However, there are some complaints about being worked too hard and too long."

"Well, Doc," said Jimmy, "this is a rehabilitation ranch, not a resort. The boys are here in order to change. We can't necessarily change their thinking, but we can change their actions. If we can make a big enough change in their actions, eventually their thinking will change. We're keeping them busy in order to change their actions."

"They say that there's no time for fun," said the doctor. "Bill said that the only fun he's had since he's been here is when you took him riding."

"Maybe they can learn to have fun while they're working. If I had a few more horses, enough where I could take everyone at once, we might be able to incorporate more fun times in our work. You might suggest to Mason that he send out a volleyball and net, or a basketball and a standard, or some baseball equipment."

"Interesting," said the doctor. "I've got to get back to the office. I'll leave these files with Emily before I go."

"Don't forget to leave the gloves and pants I left for you," said Jimmy. He tried to say that humorously, but the doctor didn't see any humor in it.

They continued to haul hay. After two and a half more days, they had the hay all stacked. Knowing that they were near finishing the hay, Emily prepared a picnic for the noon meal. They ate under the trees in front of the house.

While they were eating, Burkhart said, "There's only one more cutting, then we'll be done with the hay for this year. I always feel good when the hay work is done. I'm getting too old to do all this hard work. How do you boys feel about it?"

Nobody answered, feeling good that it was done but apprehensive about having to do more in the future.

Burkhart noticed the silence and said, "Well, I sure do appreciate your help. We got the hay up faster this year than ever before and it's because you all helped. I really appreciate it!"

Jimmy noticed that Burkhart was trying to thank the boys and pay them a compliment. He thought it might have been a little difficult for him.

"Now," said Burkhart, "I've got to go out and check my cows. How many horses and saddles you got Jimmy?"

"Right now we've got three horses and six extra saddles," replied Jimmy.

"So, to take all four of these boys riding, you need two more horses, right?"

"Yep. Dale says he's got a plan. I don't know what it is, but I'm guessing he's going to try to get us some more horses."

"Well," said Burkhart, "you bring some extra saddles and your three horses over. I have enough gentle horses we can get everyone mounted if you'd all care to help check the cattle tomorrow."

"We can do that," replied Jimmy. "Are you coming, Emily?"

"Of course she is," answered Burkhart for her. "She can use a change just like everyone else."

"I'll fix something for the noon meal," said Emily. "It will be nice to get out of the kitchen for a day. I'll ride the horse you gave me to use, Richard. The change will be nice."

Jimmy noticed that Burkhart's attitude toward the Rehabilitation Ranch seemed to be improving. He actually seemed to want to help out, other than just doing the hay cutting and baling and the irrigating.

The next morning, Jimmy saddled Digger, Max, and Killer. Emily saddled the horse Burkhart had given her to ride.

"I wonder what Richard calls this horse?" she asked. "I never thought to ask him."

Craig was selected to drive the truck with the saddles and bridles over to the Burkhart's. They drew straws to see who would ride the horses over. Holly and Mike got to ride. Shorty rode over with Craig in the truck.

As Craig started to drive away, Jimmy said, "Stay off the main road. Remember, you don't have a driver's license. And don't be in a rush. You'll get there before we do. Just wait for us. I have to adjust stirrups for Holly and Mike."

When Craig got to the Burkhart's, they found him in the corral. He'd haltered three horses and they were tied inside the corral. After a warm, friendly greeting, Burkhart said, "Pick your horses boys. They're all gentle. Get them saddled and we'll get going."

"How do you do that?" asked Bill.

"Do what?" queried Burkhart.

"Saddle them," replied Bill.

"Haven't you learned how to do that?" asked Burkhart.

"Nope," answered Bill.

"How come?" asked Burkhart.

"We've been pretty busy hauling hay and brushing colts," replied Bill.

"Well, I'll show you. Bring your saddle over here. You're Bill, aren't you?"

"Yes sir," said Bill as he went to get his saddle.

"Craig, you've already got your horse saddled. Can you help this other boy saddle his horse?"

Bill put his saddle on the ground by Burkhart. "I've already brushed these horses. When they're brushed good, you put the blanket on the horse's back, like this." He demonstrated.

"Then you place the saddle on the horses back. Like this."

He put the stirrup leather and cinches over the seat and put the saddle on the horse.

"Then, you walk around the horse and put the cinches and stirrup leather down like this."

Again, Burkhart demonstrated.

"Jimmy just throws the saddle on," said Bill.

"You can do it that way if you want," said Burkhart. "It's best to do it this way when you're learning. You stand a better chance of getting the saddle where you want it the first time. You don't want it to far forward, or too far backward. It has to be in just the right spot. Then you reach under here, get the cinch, bring it under the horse like this, and then run the latigo through the cinch ring, then back through the D ring on the saddle a couple of times."

"What's a latigo?" asked Bill.

"That's this strap here," said Burkhart, holding the latigo out.

"Then you put the tongue of the cinch ring in one of these holes in the latigo when you've got it tight enough. You don't want it too tight, but then you don't want it to loose either. Just tight enough to keep the saddle in place for the work you're doing. Got it?"

"I think so," said Bill.

"Good," said Burkhart, undoing the cinch and taking the saddle off the horse. "Now you do it!"

Bill looked a little dismayed when Burkhart took the saddle and blanket off, but re-saddled the horse the way he'd been shown. When he got done tightening the cinch, Burkhart stepped over and checked it.

"That's way too tight," he said, loosening the cinch. "This horse would have gotten a bellyache and tried to lay down after about twenty minutes. Put your fingers here and see how tight this is."

Burkhart demonstrated how much slack should be in the cinch. "No slack," he said. "Just snug. Now get your bridles. I'll show you how to properly bridle a horse."

"Bridle a horse!" said Shorty. "I want to ride him, not marry him!"

Shorty laughed at his own joke. Craig and Bill also laughed. Burkhart just grinned and said, "This is a bridle. This metal part is the bit. Most people just take the shank of the bit and try to jam it in the horse's mouth. That's not right. A horse's teeth are pretty sensitive. Hold the bit like this, on your fingers, then take your thumb and tickle his tongue, like this."

He demonstrated.

"A lot of guys will tell you to pinch his gums to get him to open his mouth. I guess you can do that, it does inflict a little pain though. I like to tickle his tongue. Most horses like to have their tongues tickled and they'll readily open their mouths for it. When the mouth is open, slip the bit in his mouth, being careful not to drag it across his teeth. When the bit is in his mouth, slide the headstall over his ears. Always bend the ears forward. Then you do up the throat latch.

Now you do it. When you've got it done, get on. We'll see how you ride."

The boys did as they were told. When they'd ridden in the corral for about five minutes, Jimmy, Emily, Holly, and Mike arrived on their horses.

"Looks like you've got my crew ready, Mister Burkhart. We're all ready, if you are."

Burkhart got on his horse, opened the gate and said, "Let's go!"

They left the corral at a walk. They paired off and talked as they rode. Emily got in the lead, next to Burkhart.

"You never told me the name of this horse, Richard. He's a good one!"

"I call him Rembrandt."

"That's a good name for him. He's pretty as a picture," said Emily. "How far do you figure on going today?"

"We'll make a circle of about ten miles. I've got a pretty good idea where most of the cattle are this time of year. I just need to make sure there are no problems that need tending to."

"What prompted you to volunteer your horses so the boys could come along?" asked Emily.

"It will do the horses some good to ride the fat off them," said Burkhart.

"Don't you think ten miles might be a little far for the boys? They've never ridden much before, if at all."

"It might be a little far, but it will toughen them up. As far as volunteering the horses, the boys worked pretty hard hauling hay. We got done quite a bit quicker than me and the Missus would have without them. I've never been much good at keeping hired help around. I tried to thank them, but I'm really not much good with words. Action speaks louder than words anyway, so this is my way of saying thanks. I'd appreciate it if you'd tell them that."

"I will," said Emily.

Jimmy was riding alongside the boys giving a few pointers on maintaining the proper posture while riding.

Before long, they came upon some cattle feeding close to a waterhole. Watching the cattle, Burkhart said, "There's one cow that's got a limp. Foot rot, I suppose. Jimmy, if I catch the head, can you get the heels?"

"I can do either one," said Jimmy.

"If I miss the head, you take it. Emily, would you keep the boys back? This might get a little western."

"What do you have to doctor her with?"

"I've got some penicillin in my saddle bag," replied Burkhart. "When we get her stretched out, I'll give her a shot."

"I can do that," said Emily.

"You ready, Jimmy? We'll just sneak up on her."

"Go for it!" said Jimmy.

Burkhart took his rope down, made a loop and slowly rode toward the lame cow. Without any fuss, he roped the cow and dallied up. She tried to get away, but Jimmy was right there ready to rope her hind feet. He only caught one foot, but dallied up anyway.

Burkhart grinned. "That's a penalty in the arena!" he said.

"It's free today, we're not in the arena! I'll get off and catch the other foot."

"Just stay on your horse," said Emily. "Give me a little slack and I'll get it for you."

Jimmy did as he was told and they had the cow stretched out, with both hind feet caught.

Emily went to Burkhart. "Got your medicine?"

"It's in the left saddle bag. The syringe and needle are in that knife scabbard."

Emily got the bottle of penicillin, the syringe and needle. "About twenty cc's?" she asked.

"That's about right," said Burkhart. "You've done this before, haven't you?"

"A few times," she said, as she filled the syringe and pressed out the air bubbles. After she had given the cow the shot, she took a sagebrush limb and scraped away the infected portion of the foot.

When she was done, she went to the cow's head and asked for slack to take the rope off.

Burkhart promptly gave her the slack she asked for. "Don't let that critter up until Emily's out of the way!" he told Jimmy.

"Don't worry," replied Jimmy. "I'm not going to let her up until Emily is back on her horse."

Emily got on her horse and Jimmy gave the cow plenty of slack. The cow kicked her way out of the rope and limped away.

"I'll come out in a day or two and see how she's doing," said Burkhart.

"I need to get this foot rot smell off," said Emily. "I'll do it in the pond over there. Smelling like this will ruin your appetite."

"I didn't bring anything to eat," said Burkhart. "I generally just go without when I'm out here."

"Don't worry," said Emily. "I brought plenty. We probably ought to get the boys off the horses and give them a rest."

"There's shade over under those aspens," said Burkhart.

"Good," said Emily. "We'll get everyone off and get them all washed up before they eat."

They went to the aspens and tied up the boys' horses. Jimmy, Emily, and Burkhart hobbled up their horses.

As they ate, they talked about the roping. The boys were impressed with the roping and Shorty asked, "Can I do that?"

"If you learn," answered Jimmy. He made a mental note to see if Mr. Mason could get ropes and a plastic steer head or he'd get them the next time he went to town.

They finished eating and continued to ride, checking the cattle.

They made a big circle and Jimmy was quick to spot the cows that carried the Grundy brand, which belonged to the Rehabilitation Ranch. He was content that they were doing well.

Later on in the afternoon, Burkhart said, "I think we've seen most all the cattle. We might as well head for home. We're not as far away as you might think."

When they got back to the Burkhart Ranch, Burkhart surprised them. "Did you boys like the horses you rode?" he asked.

The boys replied affirmatively.

"Well then, why don't you just ride them back to your place and keep them for a few days?"

"You mean you're giving us these horses?" asked Shorty.

"No, not giving them to you. Just lending them to you."

"Gee, thanks, Mister Burkhart!" The reply was the same from all the boys.

"How do you feel about that, Jimmy?" asked Burkhart.

Jimmy started to decline the offer, but noting the look of disappointment on the boy's faces, agreed. "Only if you're sure you won't be needing them. We've got plenty of feed now. Craig, can you drive the truck back? I'll lead your horse."

"I can do that," answered Craig.

"Good! Let's go home. Supper will be late tonight, we've still got our chores to do."

"Supper won't be that late. I've had it in the crock pot all day," said Emily. "It'll be ready when you've finished your chores."

Craig took the truck and the others rode out. He made it back to the ranch before the others and started doing the evening chores. When Jimmy and the others showed up, he was just finishing feeding the colts and was walking out of the corral, stopping to pet a few colts on the way.

"Playing with the colts, huh?" asked Shorty.

"Nope," said Craig. "I've just finished the evening chores. If you'll give me my horse, I'll unsaddle him." Craig took his horse from Jimmy, led him to the corral and started to unsaddle him.

When Jimmy gave Craig his horse, he said, "That's good, Craig." Then he asked the others, "How many of you would have done the evening chores if I'd have sent you back early? And without being told?"

There was silence from the boys.

"Craig is learning responsibility. That's just one thing we hope to teach you while you're here. He took care of the chores before he took care of himself. That's responsibility. If you all come over here, I'll show you how to unsaddle a horse properly.

The first thing you do is undo the latigo from the cinch. This is the latigo."

"We know," said Shorty. "Mister Burkhart showed us."

"Then," continued Jimmy, "you put the latigo through the latigo keeper like this." He demonstrated as he unsaddled Digger, then continued, "Then you walk around to the off side and hang the cinch from the cinch hanger, like this. You want this stuff put up because you don't want it dragging on the ground. When that's done, undo the throat latch on the bridle, slip it off the horse and hang it on the saddle horn. Then, take the saddle to the barn, put it on a rack and, other than turning the horse loose in the corral, you're done."

The boys started to unsaddle their horses. Jimmy asked Emily, "Do you want me to unsaddle your horse so you can go get supper started?"

"No," replied Emily, grinning. "I'm a responsible person. Supper will be ready by the time everyone gets cleaned up. It's been cooking all day."

"Okay. It looks like we're done for the day. Did the ride bother you?" asked Jimmy.

"No, not me," replied Emily. "But I suspect some of the boys are a little stiff and sore. Look at how they're walking to the bunkhouse."

Jimmy watched the boys as they went to the bunkhouse. They all appeared to have gotten a little stiff from being in the saddle all day and not being used to it.

"They'll toughen up," said Jimmy.

"It's a good thing I went with you today," said Emily.

"How come?"

"You and Richard would have rode all day without stopping to eat," said Emily. "That's too much for those young boys. You need to be a little more considerate of them and not so concerned with doing the job at hand. I'll talk with Richard next time I see him, or Louise."

"I'll remember that," said Jimmy. "I need to call Mason to see if he can get some used ropes and a steer head at the saddle shop. We might keep these boys busy and have some fun teaching them how to rope."

After supper that night, Jimmy called Mason at his home.

"What kind of problem do you have, calling me at home?" said Mason as he answered the phone.

"None," said Jimmy, laughing. "I just need a little favor."

"Favor? What is it?"

"I need five or six used lariat ropes and …"

"Lariat ropes! What are you going to do, hang those boys?" interrupted Mason.

"No," said Jimmy, still laughing. "We're going to teach them how to rope. If anybody gets hanged, they'll hang themselves. We also need a steer head we can stick into a bale of hay. You can get everything at the saddle shop. The last time I was there, they had plenty of ropes and they were only a couple of bucks apiece. You can bring them or send them out next time anybody comes."

"I'll do it, but don't know when," replied Mason.

Visitors

With the hay hauling done, the boys had plenty of time to mess with the colts and there was enough time in the afternoon to ride for a couple of hours. During these horseback rides, Jimmy gave each one of the boy's hints on how to improve their riding. The more they rode, the better they got, although they were a long way from being expert. They got to the point where they looked forward to riding each day. Soon Jimmy had them trotting in the corral, trying to master the rhythm of the trot. Bill and Holly had a hard time at the trot and each one of them fell off. They weren't hurt, just embarrassed. Bill was even able to laugh at himself a little.

Dale Williams returned.

"How was your trip?" asked Jimmy.

"Not successful," replied Dale.

"Where did you go and what did you do?"

"I went over to the Wilson Ranch and visited with Bud, Pat, and Honey. By the way, they all said to say hello."

"How are they doing?"

"They're having the busiest year ever according to Pat," replied Dale. "They've had to hire extra wranglers."

"What did you go over there for?" asked Jimmy.

"I thought I could talk them into donating a few horses for this place," said Dale.

"Ha!" exclaimed Jimmy. "I was over there earlier this year when I went to get my horse, Digger. Honey volunteered to donate Max. That's how he got here. I wish you'd have told me your plans,

I could have saved you a trip. Honey told me they were expecting a busy year and might even have to buy some extra horses for themselves."

"I know," said Dale, "I ended up riding some colts for them."

"I guess it was a good try," said Jimmy. "But you still did good, for you."

"How do you mean?"

"You missed the rest of the hay hauling," said Jimmy, with a grin on his face.

Dale grinned and turned to leave. "I'll be ready for anything in the morning."

Jimmy grinned as Dale left. *I can't blame him for wanting to miss out on the hay hauling,* he thought. *He's a volunteer and I can't really force him to do anything.*

One day, Mason showed up. He had some used ropes and a plastic steer head, along with a volleyball and a net.

"You asked for these," he said, as he handed the ropes and steer head to Jimmy. "Emily asked for these." He handed the net and volleyball to Jimmy.

"She told me she had talked with you on the phone."

"We have some family members that want to visit their youngsters," said Mason. "Namely, Michael Thornton's folks. How do you feel about family visits?"

"I don't have any thoughts one way or another about it," replied Jimmy. "We're not really set up to accommodate visitors overnight or to provide meals for them."

"I understand that," replied Mason. "I wonder if it would do any good for the youngsters' moral."

"That probably depends on the youngster," said Jimmy. "Before we let parents or visitors come, maybe we should do some sort of background check on them. Perhaps the final decision should come from the youngsters themselves. How much of each boy's problems are due to the parents or their lack of involvement in their child's life?"

"There's some good points to ponder," said Mason. "We'll take them into consideration. But, I don't see any harm in letting immediate family members out for a short visit."

"You see how Mike feels about it, and we'll go from there."

"Maybe we ought to call a meeting of all the boys and pose the question to them," said Mason.

"Yes," answered Jimmy. "We can do it at dinner. You'll stay and eat with us, of course."

"I better, just to see how this is going to turn out."

After dinner, Mason asked the boys, "How do you feel about your parents occasionally coming out to visit for a few hours?"

There was silence from all the boys.

Mason, feeling a little uncomfortable, asked Holly, "How do you feel about it?"

Holly replied, "It don't make no difference to me."

"Doesn't make any difference to me," corrected Mason. "Mike, how do you feel about it?"

"I could care less one way or the other," answered Mike.

"Shorty, what about you?"

"My folks wouldn't come out if they had a free ride! They don't care what happens to me. And I don't care what happens to them!"

"Hum," said Mason. "Bill, how do you feel?"

"I wouldn't mind seeing my mom," answered Bill. "But I really don't want to see my dad."

"So you're a real mommy's boy, huh?" said Shorty.

"No," replied Bill. "But my dad used to beat me pretty bad. I don't want to see him."

"Well," said Mason, "Mike, your folks have asked about coming out for a visit. Are you okay with that?"

"As I said, I could care less one way or the other."

Frustrated to some degree, Mason said, "We'll arrange for a short visit and see how it goes. I'll tell your folks they can come out next Sunday for a few hours."

When the boys went to the barn to saddle their horses, Mason said to Jimmy, "I was really disappointed with the response I got. I thought the boys would be anxious to see their families."

"Well," said Jimmy, "you need to remember these boys either come from broken homes or there's problems at home that have contributed to their delinquency. We'll see how it goes."

The following Sunday, Mike's parents showed up. They brought his uncle and younger brother. Mike introduced them to Jimmy and the other boys.

Jimmy explained, "We can't take you riding or anything like that, but you're welcome to have Mike show you around the ranch. You only have a couple of hours, have a good visit. I have some work to do with the other boys. I'll see you before you go."

Jimmy left to take the other boys for the afternoon ride. Dale and Emily joined them. On the trail, Emily asked, "Do you think it's a good idea to leave them alone, unsupervised?"

"I don't see what harm can come from it," said Jimmy. "Mike's with his parents and they consented with Judge Reynolds to have him come out here."

When the riders returned to the ranch, they found the Thornton family ready to leave. Jimmy joined them after he unsaddled his horse.

"I hope you folks had a nice visit with Mike," said Jimmy.

"It was very nice," said Missus Thornton. "Michael showed us all over the place."

"This is a neat place!" said Mike's little brother. "I'd like to come out here and live!"

Jimmy just grinned. He judged the youngster to be about eight or nine. It was clear that he had no idea why his brother was out here.

"Thanks for the opportunity to visit Michael," said Missus Thornton.

"Yeah, thanks," said Mister Thornton.

Mike's uncle was noncommittal. They got in the car and drove off.

Strange family, thought Jimmy as he watched them go.

Two days later, about one o'clock in the morning, Jimmy was awakened by Craig.

"You better come down to the bunkhouse, Jimmy! We've got some trouble."

"What's the matter?" asked Jimmy, as he pulled on his pants.

"Mike!" answered Craig. "He's high as a kite and threatening everyone! He's acting real crazy!"

"Better come down, Dale!" ordered Jimmy, as he put on his hat and started toward the bunkhouse.

As Jimmy left the house, Emily came from her room, tying a housecoat around her. "What's going on?" she asked as she followed Jimmy and Craig to the bunkhouse.

"Don't know. You better wait here," said Jimmy as he entered the bunkhouse. The boys were in various stages of undress.

"What's going on here?" he demanded.

"Mike, he's gone nuts," said Shorty.

Mike was standing on a bunk, holding a knife in one hand and waving it around in an erratic manner, and threatening everyone that tried to approach. Even though it was just a butter knife, it was still a knife. In the other hand, he held some sort of cigarette. Jimmy could tell he was high on something, but he didn't know what.

He started talking to Mike in a low, soothing voice, like he talked to the colts. Not getting a positive response, he told everyone to leave the room. He tried to talk to Mike, but his efforts were unsuccessful.

Mike continued to smoke the cigarette and make threats to everyone, even though Jimmy was the only one present. Jimmy could see that he was clearly out of his head.

Jimmy's only hope was that Mike would pass out. He knew that a lot of addicts, when they're high seem to have almost super human strength. Jimmy wondered if he could restrain him alone even if he could get the butter knife from him.

"Dale! Come in here. I might need some help!"

"I'm right behind you," answered Dale.

"I'm kinda at a loss at what to do," said Jimmy. "We need to get that knife away from him before he hurts himself or someone else."

"Maybe we can approach him from two different sides," said

Dale. "We might get a hold of him that way. I'll go around from his left, you go around from the right."

Before they approached Mike, he got a strange look on his face and fell to the floor, unconscious. Fortunately, he didn't fall on the knife.

"Get the knife, quick, Dale!"

"No need to hurry," replied Dale. "He's passed out. Put him on his bunk."

"Emily!" called Jimmy.

From outside the bunkhouse, Craig answered. "She went to the house to call the sheriff."

"Tell her to have them send out an ambulance. We have some sort of drug overdose here. And tell them to hurry!"

A half an hour later, two sheriff's deputies and an ambulance showed up. The EMT's attended to Mike. They put him on a stretcher and loaded him in the ambulance.

One of the sheriffs came over to Jimmy and asked, "Are you in charge here?"

"Yes sir," replied Jimmy. "Craig woke me up and said that Mike was high on something and threatening everyone. When I got here, he was standing on a bunk with the knife in one hand and some sort of smoke in the other. Before Dale and I could restrain him, he passed out. Look! His cigarette is on the floor, still burning."

The deputy picked up the half-burnt cigarette, put it out, and put it in an envelope.

"Evidence," said the deputy. "How'd he get this?"

"I really don't know," said Jimmy. "He didn't have it when he came a few weeks ago. His folks did come out for a visit last Sunday."

"Who are his folks?"

Jimmy answered all the questions from the deputy. When he was done, he said, "We'll need to question all the boys here before we leave."

"Sure," said Jimmy. "We might as well go to the house to finish up. I'll have Emily make some coffee. Get dressed boys, we're going to the house."

Emily had already started the coffee. She poured Jimmy, Dale, and the two officers each a cup. "There's cream and sugar on the table," she said.

"I'll need to question each one of the boys alone," said the officer in charge. "Is there a place I can do that?"

"My office is right there," said Jimmy. "Use it."

The sheriff questioned each boy one at a time in the office. Then he questioned Emily and Dale. When he got done, he asked for another cup of coffee and said, "Everyone is in agreement as to what happened and everyone seems to think that his parents smuggled him the dope. It's hard to believe that parents would actively support their child's drug habit. But it does happen."

"His uncle was with his folks when they came for the visit, and a younger brother."

"Do you know the uncle's name?" asked the sheriff.

"No," said Jimmy. "The uncle didn't say anything at all. He didn't even say hello when he was introduced to us."

"We'll find out who the uncle is," said the sheriff. "It's almost daylight. We've been here longer than I expected. Thank you all for your cooperation."

The deputies started to leave and Emily asked, "Do you want some coffee to go?"

"No thank you, ma'am. We've had plenty."

The sheriffs left.

"Well, boys" said Jimmy. "It's too late to go back to bed. What do you say, we start early then quit early this afternoon?"

The answer was affirmative from all the boys.

"We can do the morning chores while Emily fixes breakfast. Let's go."

After the chores were done and during breakfast, Jimmy tried to answer questions the boys had regarding the incident. The most common question was regarding Mike.

"What are they going to do with him?" "Is he going to jail?" "Will he come back here?" These were the questions the boys asked, in various forms. At this point in time, Jimmy didn't know the answers.

After breakfast, Jimmy sent Dale and the boys to the corrals to mess with the colts. At eight o'clock, he called Mason.

When Mason answered the phone, Jimmy said, "We had a little incident out here last night."

"What happened?" asked Mason.

Jimmy related the events of the previous night. When he got done, he said, "I suppose Mike's in the hospital now. I would suggest you contact them and not allow them to release Mike to his parents. They're the only ones that could have got the drugs to him."

"Yes," said Mason. "I'll have to look into this closer."

"Would you let me know what's happening?" asked Jimmy.

"I'll keep you posted as I find out anything," said Mason.

"You know," said Jimmy, "That's a real shame. Mike seemed to be doing well."

"Yes. You know, this will put an end to family visits. Maybe that wasn't such a hot idea to start with."

Mason hung up the phone and called the hospital to check on the status of Mike.

Jimmy went to the corrals to help with the colts.

A week later, Mason showed up at the ranch.

"Do you have any news about Mike, Mister Mason?" asked Shorty.

"Yes, I do. I'll tell you all at dinner."

As they ate, Mason told the latest news about Mike. "He was in the hospital for three days, then released to a treatment center on Judge Reynolds order."

"A treatment center?" questioned Bill. "They treat drug addiction with addicting drugs. They're no good."

"How do you know, Bill?"

"Because I've been to one. I don't really like them."

"It sounds like to me you want to stay clean and sober," said Mason.

"Yes sir!" replied Bill.

"Well, Mike will be there until he's released."

"Then what happens?" asked Holly.

"I don't really know," replied Mason. "I talked with him after he got checked into the treatment center. He said he really wants to come back here and that he'll miss the horse riding."

"I'll bet he doesn't miss the hay hauling," said Shorty.

"Actually, he said he'd even miss that."

"Can he come back here?" asked Holly.

"That depends on the judge. You know he told all of you that this was essentially your last chance before he sent you here. If we let this sort of thing go on without any consequences, the judge's decisions won't carry much weight. I very seriously doubt that he'll be allowed back here. His actions have seriously jeopardized this program and all of your futures also. Hopefully, this will amount to a good wake-up call for all of you. Jimmy, I need to talk with you privately for a spell."

"Boys, go saddle your horses. I'll be down shortly."

When the boys had left, Mason said to Jimmy, "Mike told me it was his uncle that supplied him with the drugs. He's been supplying him with them for quite some time. The judge has issued an order for his arrest, and we found out that there's a few other warrants out for him. The judge wanted me to alert you to the fact that the uncle might suspect that you fingered him in this deal. Be wary of any strangers showing up. I'm having some signs printed up that should keep trespassers off the property, and I'll get them out to you as soon as I can. Do you have any questions?"

"No," said Jimmy. "I just hope Mike's okay."

"I'll keep you posted. I'm going back to the office and see if I can recommend another youngster to take Mike's place. I've got a few boys in mind. I'll be talking to you. I need to take Mike's file, he's done here. By the way, where did you get the extra horses?"

As Jimmy got Mike's file, he answered Mason's question. "Richard Burkhart lent us a few. He's turning out to be a better neighbor than I thought he'd be," said Jimmy. "If you send extra boys, I'd only send one, that's all the horses we have now."

"Right," replied Mason, and he left.

The days were getting shorter as fall was approaching.

One day while out riding, Jimmy and the boys rode over to the Burkhart's. They found him cutting the third crop of hay. When they approached, he turned off the swather to visit.

"Getting it cut down, are you?" asked Jimmy.

"Yep. It's that time. I'll be ready to start hauling in two days. Are you going to help haul again?"

"Yes sir," replied Jimmy. "That is our deal."

"I'll be ready to start early."

"We'll be here."

Two days later, Jimmy and the boys were up early, ready to haul hay. The boys didn't really look forward to hauling hay, but Jimmy told them, "That's part of the job. The sooner we get started, the sooner we'll be done."

Jimmy was taken by surprise when Shorty said, "That's what Craig says."

Apparently, Craig had been listening earlier.

The hay hauling went as well as could be expected. There wasn't as much complaining from the boys as there had been before, as they were getting in better physical shape. Dale helped out every day. He couldn't find an excuse to leave.

When Burkhart's hay was hauled he came over and started cutting the Rehabilitation Ranch's hay. The boys were quite relieved when the hay hauling was done.

When the hay was put up, Jimmy had the boys dig two post holes in a level, unused part of the yard. They set a tall pine post in each hole.

"What's that for?" asked Bill.

"We'll set up a volleyball net and have a few games of volleyball," replied Jimmy.

"Volleyball? That's a girl's game!" said Shorty.

"It might be," said Jimmy, "But it is fun. You'll see."

They set up the net and took a day to relax and play volleyball. Surprisingly, the boys enjoyed the game. Jimmy and Dale joined in the game with each one being on opposing sides. They were taller than the boys. Shorty was the surprise. Although he was shorter than the other boys, he was very aggressive at the game.

Because the boys took readily to the game, Jimmy decided to have a game every night before supper. *All work and no play makes a delinquent more of a delinquent,* he thought.

One day, as the weather was turning cooler, Burkhart came to the ranch on his four-wheeler. Jimmy met him at the corrals and after greeting each of the boys, he said, "I figure we've got about another month before we have to start gathering cattle. Do you and the boys want to help?"

"Do we get a chance to be real cowboys?" asked Holly.

"Only if Jimmy here agrees," answered Burkhart.

"I think we could help you, but I don't know how much help the boys will be," replied Jimmy. "They've never been around cattle before."

"Many hands make light work," replied Burkhart. "They'd need to dress real warm. It gets cold on the mountain this time of year."

"I think we can help out," said Jimmy.

There was an undercurrent of excitement among the boys as they anticipated the gathering of the cattle. None of them had ever been around cattle at any time in their lives. All they knew about cattle was what they'd seen in the movies.

The New Hand

While they were awaiting the fall gather, Mason showed up with signs that read, "STATE PROPERTY—NO ADMITTANCE." There was a long list of fines and jail terms listed below advising the potential violator of the consequences of entering the property without permission.

He also brought another boy to stay at the ranch. His name was Timothy Clark. He was a typical juvenile delinquent. He'd been caught with some drugs while trying to steal some cigarettes. Like all the previous new arrivals, he seemed quiet and sullen when he arrived.

Jimmy looked over his papers as Mason told him about the boy. There wasn't anything spectacular or outstanding about him, just another delinquent that had got off on the wrong foot.

When he finished looking over Timothy's papers, he stuck out his hand and said, "I'm Jimmy, Timothy."

"Just Tim," answered the boy.

"You can shake Jimmy's hand, Mister Clark," said Mason.

Reluctantly, Tim held out his hand and meekly shook Jimmy's hand.

Jimmy called the other boys over, introduced Tim to them and said, "You boys can help take Tim's stuff into the bunkhouse. It's in Mister Mason's car."

Jimmy noticed that Tim didn't shake the boy's hands when they were introduced.

"Not comfortable in the social skills," he said to Mason, as he mentioned it to him.

"Either that or he's painfully bashful or shy," said Mason.

"I have a question for you," said Jimmy.

"What is it? Shoot," answered Mason.

"School is about to start. What are we going to do about sending these boys to school?"

"Don't worry about it," replied Mason. "They have all been expelled from their schools. With their records, they'd all have a hard time enrolling in any school, even a military academy. Hopefully, you can teach them how to get along in society and they can complete their education at a later date."

"Okay," said Jimmy. "I just wanted to make sure. But they don't seem that tough out here."

"They're out of their element here. The real test will come when they leave here and return to society, so to speak. If you can get them to do some reading or even write letters to their folks, it might prove helpful," said Mason.

"You'd better send out some books, there's nothing to read here."

"Where shall I get books, much less the money to buy them?" asked Mason.

"Go to the library. Quite often they sell books. Or go to a used bookstore. They generally have a discounted sale table," replied Jimmy.

"Good idea," said Mason. "By the way, don't be surprised to see some deputy sheriffs occasionally. They haven't caught Mike's uncle yet and the judge and county sheriff are concerned he might show up here wanting to get even for you fingering him."

"But I didn't finger him," said Jimmy.

"I know," said Mason. "But Mike's uncle doesn't know that. We can't be too careful. If there's anyone hanging around, let the sheriff know. They'll be out as soon as they can. Be sure to put up those signs, one on each side of the road coming into the ranch. Anything you need, in addition to books?"

"Can't think of anything, other than some long johns and winter clothing for the boys. It's liable to get cold pretty soon," answered Jimmy.

"That's right," said Mason. "I don't know what to do about clothes and the proper sizes. You better plan on bringing them into town to get clothes."

"There's too many people to fit into one vehicle. We'd have to make more than one trip," said Jimmy. "And I don't think we have enough money to go to the department store."

"You're right," replied Mason. "I'll see about getting a van from the state. As far as clothes shopping is concerned, maybe we could take them to the Goodwill Store or a second-hand store. We might save some money at one of those places. I'll look into it and let you know. Make a list of what each boy needs."

"Yes sir," replied Jimmy.

Mason left and Jimmy went to the bunkhouse. "Are you getting settled in, Tim?" he asked.

"I guess so," answered Tim.

"You'll need to keep your area clean and in shape," said Jimmy. "Craig here is the bunkhouse boss, he'll show you."

"What do you do here?" asked Tim.

"We're taking young, wild horses, colts actually, and …"

"What's a colt?" asked Tim.

"A colt is a young horse." Jimmy could see he was going to have to start from square one with Tim. But then he had a pleasant thought, *Perhaps the other boys could help!*

"With these young horses," continued Jimmy, "we're teaching them how to get along with people. In teaching them that, they might teach you boys some things about getting along with people also. It's kind of a two-way street. Right now, we have eight colts that we've gentled down, halter broke, and taught how to lead. We've been spending a lot of time brushing them and teaching them to trust us."

Jimmy then called all the boys together and said, "Tim here is new and hasn't been around horses before. I need you to help him and bring him up to speed. You'll need to show him how to catch a colt, halter him, brush him—show him all the things you've learned since you've been here. Tomorrow, we'll give him some riding lessons, starting with saddling and bridling. You'll all be expected to demonstrate. Can you do that?"

The boys answered affirmatively. Jimmy thought that the addition of a new youngster might be beneficial to the other boys and make his job easier. *If I can use the other boys to help the newcomer, it might be good for all of them,* he thought. *I'll just have to supervise.*

After supper that night, Jimmy told his plan to Emily. She approved and then said, "You might work this deal into something where you don't have to do anything at all, just supervise. You'll get fat, just sitting around!"

Jimmy laughed. "I don't think it will become that easy, but it would be nice if it did."

The next morning, Tim assisted in doing the morning chores.

"He don't do much!" complained Shorty. "Mostly just watches."

"That's all right," replied Jimmy. "I'm told that in the army, when they teach you something, they tell you then they show you, then they have you do it. We're kinda using the same method here. Are you telling Tim what you're doing and why?"

"Not exactly," replied Shorty.

"It's important not only to tell everyone what we're doing, but why. Reasons are important," said Jimmy.

When the chores were done, Jimmy had the boys saddle and bridle their horses, giving Tim instruction as they did it. He had to correct Bill once.

"Rather than saying 'take this thing and put it through here,' say take this latigo, put it through the cinch ring then put it through the 'D' ring," said Jimmy. "You can teach the parts of a saddle as you're teaching how to do something. Kinda like killing two birds with one stone."

Jimmy had Tim saddle his horse, then checked the cinch. "This needs to be just a little tighter," he said, as he pulled the cinch up a couple of holes. "You want it snug enough to keep the saddle in place. Now we'll have a little riding lesson and each one of these boys can demonstrate for you."

During the riding lesson, Jimmy had each one of the boys demonstrate something and explain to Tim what he was doing. Then he had Tim do it. After an appropriate amount of time in the corral, they headed out, with Jimmy leading. He heard the boys giving Tim some help as they went along. He thought, *Maybe I ought to follow and watch. Make sure the boys are helping rather than hindering Tim.*

"Holly," he said, "you come up here and lead."

"But I don't know where we're going!" replied Holly.

"We're headed to the forest and checking the water holes along the way," replied Jimmy.

"Oh," said Holly. He took the lead.

The ride was more for enjoyment than work and the group didn't find anything amiss. When they got to the forest, the wire gate was closed. Holly stopped.

"Get off and open it," said Jimmy. "Then when everybody gets through it, close it."

"Oh," said Holly. He got off his horse and opened the gate. As each one of the boys passed through it they had a remark for Holly.

"I appreciate your service," said Bill. "You're a good servant!"

"I've never had a butler before," said Shorty. "I'd appreciate breakfast in bed tomorrow. Eggs over easy, ham, toast, and coffee!"

"Fat chance!" replied Holly.

Tim simply said, "Thanks."

Jimmy rode through the gate and said, "Now close it."

He was having a hard time closing the gate and after giving him enough time to get it done, Jimmy said, "You boys turn your horses around and I'll show you how to close a wire gate."

Jimmy got off his horse and started to close the gate. As he did, he explained what he was doing. "First, straighten the gate by pulling it. Then, put the bottom of this stay into the wire loop at the bottom. Then put your shoulder on the top of this post and reach the gatepost with your hand. Then pull the gate to the gatepost until you can slip this loop over the stay. Then it's done. Each one of you boys will have a chance to try it. We'll come along later and make some cheaters to make it easier."

He opened the gate and said, "Now you do it Holly."

Holly did as he was told and said, "That was easier than the way I was trying to do it."

"Bill, you lead," said Jimmy.

"Where are we going?"

"Go to the second water hole, then go to the south. We'll circle back to the ranch. We need to get back in time to do the chores and have supper."

4-H

Bill started out. Along the way they saw some of Missus Grundy's cows and calves. The boys stopped to look over the cattle. They all looked to be in pretty good shape.

"Do you think there are any 4-H club calves in that bunch?" asked Jimmy.

"What's 4-H?" asked Bill.

"4-H is a program for youngsters where they raise their club calves, sheep, or pigs to show and compete in the county fair against other youngsters in the 4-H projects," said Jimmy. "They sell the animals at the 4-H sale and use the money to go to college or whatever."

"What does 4-H stand for?" asked Holly.

"If I remember right, it's head, heart, hands, and health," answered Jimmy. "We'll enroll each one of you guys in 4-H and you can participate in the program. You can each select a calf after we round them up and wean them. You'll have to gentle them down, teach them to lead and stand, just like you did with the colts."

The end of summer drew near and the boys anxiously awaited the day they were to start gathering cattle. There were an awful lot of questions about the 4-H projects they would be starting. One of the questions was "Where is 4-H held?"

Jimmy hadn't given any thought about the kids going to 4-H club meetings and wasn't sure how to answer the question. He let the question slide for the time being, deciding that he'd better call the county extension agent and get information about where the meetings were held.

The next day, during the noon break, he called the extension agent. His name was Harold Turner.

Jimmy explained what he was looking for and Harold told him what was required. "The calves will need to be ear tagged and identified. The youngsters will need to keep accurate records about the animals. We supply record books for that."

Jimmy asked, "What about the meetings?"

"The meetings are held every few weeks during the winter here at the extension office. We try to have a guest speaker, a vet or a nutritionist or someone like that from the college to help teach the kids every time we meet. We'll generally provide some punch and cookies."

"The extension office is quite a ways away from where we are and I've got four boys we want to enroll in the program and just one pickup. I don't have a way to haul them into town."

"Just where are you?" asked the agent.

Jimmy explained that they were out at the old Grundy place. "We're the Juvenile Delinquent Rehabilitation Ranch."

"Ah, yes," said the agent. "I've heard a little something about your program. How's it working out?"

"So far, so good," said Jimmy. "But it's going to be a little difficult to get the youngsters into town for the club meetings every few weeks."

"The 4-H program is good for youngsters. It teaches responsibility and service. Why don't you start your own club out there?" asked the agent.

"That's an interesting idea," said Jimmy. "I wouldn't have thought of it. What's required?"

"I'll tell you what," replied the agent. "When I come out to ear tag the calves, I'll bring out everything you need and we can get acquainted. I'd be interested in seeing what you're doing."

"Good," said Jimmy. "We'll be gathering cattle soon and the boys can pick out their own calves. I'll call you when that's done and we'll set up a time and date for you to come out."

The boys continued to work with the colts as fall approached.

They rode every day and some of them thought they were becoming quite accomplished horsemen. Jimmy noticed this attitude and told the boys, "You've got a long way to go until you become accomplished horsemen!"

Jimmy's comment didn't diminish the enthusiasm the boys had for horseback riding. Tim was the only one that didn't seem to relish riding. He was generally the last one to get his horse saddled every day and the last one to get mounted when they were ready to ride. The other boys ribbed Tim about his lack of enthusiasm for riding, but he didn't have a reply for his tardiness. He just let the boys rib him.

Jimmy saw that Tim wasn't really fitting in with the group, but decided not to say or do anything about it at this time. He wondered privately if Tim might have some mental problems that prohibited his mixing in with the others.

One day, after a few days of a light snowfall, Mason showed up driving a van. The van was marked with the sheriff's department decals and had expanded metal on the inside of the windows. The driver's compartment was enclosed with expanded metal.

"What's up?" asked Jimmy, as Mason got out of the van. The boys joined Jimmy as he greeted Mason. They each shook hands with him.

"We're all going to town to get the group some winter clothing," replied Mason. "I imagine you boys are getting a little cold in the mornings."

"Isn't that what they used to call a 'paddy wagon,'" asked Shorty.

"Yes," replied Mason. "They still do."

"Well, I ain't riding in it. It's for jailbirds!" said Shorty.

"Me either!" joined in Bill and Holly.

"It's either ride in it to town, or freeze during the winter without any winter clothes," said Mason. He wasn't giving the boys much in the way of options.

"I'll ride in it," said Tim. "I've been in one before. We won't be handcuffed, will we?"

Mason laughed. "No," he answered. Then he added, still laughing, "Not unless you want to be."

With Tim's willingness to ride in the paddy wagon, the other boys entered the van. When Jimmy joined them in the van, they relaxed a little more.

Mason asked Emily, who had joined the group, "Do you want to ride to town with us?"

"No," replied Emily. "Dale and I will ride to town in my car."

On the way to town, Mason explained, "We're going to town to get winter clothing. You boys want to get clothes that will keep you warm and not necessarily in the current fashion. Nobody is going to see you out there on the ranch."

On the way, Jimmy and Mason discussed Jimmy's plans to establish a 4-H club for the boys. Mason thought it was a good idea.

"Of course," said Jimmy, "if we had a van like this, we could join the existing club in town and attend their meetings."

"That's right," said Mason. "But we don't have a van. I only borrowed this from the sheriff's department for today. Establishing a club out there on the ranch is a better idea."

When they got to town, they went to the Goodwill Store. Although the clothing items in the store were used, they were clean and serviceable. Before they went in, Mason told the boys, "You boys be on your best behavior, we'll be watching you."

Mason led the group into the store and directly to where the winter coats were. "We'll start here."

The boys started looking over the offerings and almost immediately there was an argument between Shorty and Tim over a coat. Jimmy noticed this and said to the boys, "Gentlemen, there will be no arguments while we're in town. Shorty, try this coat, that one's a little large for you."

Reluctantly, Shorty tried on the coat Jimmy suggested. "Yeah, this one will work."

When the boys had selected their coats, they went to the shirts and picked out winter shirts. Thus went the day. The boys selected everything they thought they needed for winter clothing, right down to long johns.

Emily and Dale joined them before they checked out their clothing. As they were checking out, Emily made the comment to Holly, "Aren't you forgetting the gloves you put in the pocket of the coat?"

"Oh, yeah!" exclaimed Holly, obviously embarrassed. "I forgot."

Jimmy was watching and thought, *There's still a little larceny in these youngsters. We have a long way to go.*

"Dale," asked Jimmy, "aren't you going to get any winter clothes?"

"No," replied Dale. "I thought I'd drift farther south for the winter where it's not so cold."

Jimmy just shrugged his shoulders. Dale was volunteer help and probably wanted to find work where he was paid for his labors.

When the shopping was done, Mason said, "We'll eat in town then head home. Do you have everything you need?"

The answers were affirmative.

After supper, they returned to the ranch.

Gathering Cattle

The next few days were spent handling the colts in the morning and riding in the afternoon. Snow started to fall and the temperature steadily dropped at night, although the afternoons were fairly warm.

One day, Burkhart showed up. "I'm thinking I'll start gathering cattle day after tomorrow," he told Jimmy. "Are you going to help?"

"We sure are," replied Shorty, not giving Jimmy a chance to answer.

"Some of the cows have started drifting off the mountain," said Burkhart. "I imagine it's getting kinda cold up there. I could sure use your help if you're a mind to."

Jimmy thought that Burkhart might be depending on the boys at the Juvenile Rehabilitation Ranch for help. He wasn't alarmed by the thought, even though the help was free. But it did give the boys some extra duties and the opportunity to be of service. He thought it might actually be helping the boys.

"When do you want to get started?" asked Jimmy.

"We need to get started early, before sunup."

"If we were to be at your place by six, would that be early enough?" asked Jimmy.

"That should be early enough," replied Burkhart.

The next day was filled with anticipation about the following day and the boys becoming real cowboys. That night, Jimmy told the group, "Hit the sack early. We've got to get up early, do our chores and be over at Burkhart's by six. Dress warm tomorrow, it'll be cold that early in the morning."

The next morning, Jimmy was up about four-thirty and surprised to find the boys already up and dressed. "We'll do our chores, eat breakfast, then head out," he said.

When the chores were done, breakfast eaten, and they were ready to start out, Emily gave each one of the boys a sack lunch. They went to the barn, saddled their horses and started out. Emily and Dale joined them.

They got to the Burkhart Ranch shortly after six.

"Sorry we're a little late," Jimmy told Burkhart. He was in the house sipping on an extra cup of coffee.

"Just right," said Burkhart. "Had your breakfast?"

"Yes," replied Jimmy.

"My horse is saddled in the barn. We'll get mounted and go."

As they rode to the mountain, at a trot, Jimmy explained to Burkhart, "I kinda got it figured that we'll keep a boy between each one of the adults and pretty well keep each one in sight. Hopefully, we won't lose anybody."

"Good idea," said Burkhart. "How do you want to divide them up?"

"We'll start with Dale, then Shorty, then Holly, then Emily, then Bill, then me, then Tim, then Craig, then you. You tell each rider where to go and when to start."

"Sounds good to me," said Burkhart. "We'll meet at the gate we just came through and take the cattle to the hayfields. I'll need to get a count on them before we turn them loose."

As the sun was coming up, and they approached the top of the mountain, Burkhart started dropping off riders, telling each one where to go and where they could expect to meet up. Jimmy told each rider to keep the riders on either side of him in sight, then, if someone needed some help, he could help out.

Burkhart told each rider to wait until he gave a loud holler or until the adjoining rider gave a signal to start. He also told them to bring every cow they found.

Finally, Burkhart and Craig were the last riders. "Craig, you start here and keep a close eye on Tim. I'm pretty sure I won't get lost!"

Craig laughed and waited until Burkhart yelled. He then signaled Tim and the signal went all the way to Dale. They started. The cattle roundup had begun. The riders started moving.

Where they had started at a trot, when they started to gather cattle, they moved at a walk.

Holly was the first to find cattle and slowly but surely the others found cattle. Jimmy lost sight of Tim once when he went into a draw to push out some cows and calves, but when he had them headed toward the other cattle he'd gathered, he saw Tim. He also saw Craig, pushing a fairly large bunch of cattle. Craig appeared to be having a hard time, so Jimmy rode over to Tim and sent him to help Craig.

"I really don't know what to do," said Tim.

"Just get behind the cows and keep them moving down the mountain," said Jimmy. "Craig could use some help."

Sending Tim to help Craig gave Jimmy more ground to cover, but he thought he could handle it. He headed the cattle he'd already gathered toward where Craig was headed, and went back to where he could see Bill.

Bill and Emily were working together, moving a sizeable bunch of cattle. Jimmy went back to riding the ground he was supposed to be riding plus that which Tim was supposed to be covering. *So far, so good,* he thought.

As the riders pushed the cattle toward the gate, they started meeting. They ate their sack lunches as they moved and about one o'clock they had all arrived at the gate. Burkhart opened the gate to the hayfields, got on his horse and started counting the cattle as they went through the gate. Jimmy moved up close to the gate so he could slow down the cattle, making it easier for Burkhart to get an accurate count.

When the cattle were all through the gate and counted, Burkhart got out his tally book and wrote the number down. "We're short about seventy-three head according to my count," he said.

"Seventy-two," said Dale. "I came across a dead cow up on the ridge. I couldn't tell, but it looked like she'd been struck by lightning."

"Well, tomorrow we'll ride to the southeast and gather that part of the range," said Burkhart. "That is if you boys are up to it! It'll be harder than today."

"Harder than today?" exclaimed Tim. "There couldn't be anything harder than today!"

"Of course we're up to it," said Shorty. "We're real cowboys now!"

They rode back to Burkhart's ranch. "You are going to stay for supper," said Burkhart. It was more like a command than an invitation. "The Missus has figured on it!"

Emily started to object, but Jimmy stopped her. "We'd be honored," he said.

"But you'll be doing the chores after dark," said Emily.

"We can handle it," replied Jimmy.

After supper at the Burkhart's, the crew rode home in the dark.

"It's kinda spooky riding in the dark," said Bill.

"You're afraid of the dark!" said Shorty.

"No," said Bill. "It's just different."

"Just trust your horse," said Jimmy. "Their night vision is generally better than ours."

The ride back to the Rehabilitation Ranch was quiet. The boys we tired. They got to the ranch, unsaddled their horses and did the chores.

Jimmy admonished them, "Hit the sack. We've got another early day tomorrow and it's liable to be harder riding."

The next day, the boys were up early again, even though they'd put in a pretty rough day previously. Tim was a little slow moving.

They arrived at the Burkhart's earlier than before. "We'll do things a little different today," said Burkhart, as they started out toward the southeast. "We'll split up by twos and cover the ground. The country is rougher."

Burkhart started scattering the riders shortly after sunup. With an adult accompanying each youngster, it wasn't necessary to keep in sight of each other. Burkhart told each rider where they could expect to meet and form the herd to take to the hayfields.

He indicated that the first riders were to wait until the other riders showed up with their cattle. They'd use the fence to keep the cattle lined out in the right direction.

The day wore on. Emily had fixed some sack lunches again and they were eaten in the saddle on the go. The groups didn't gather as many cattle as they did the day before, and the country was rougher than the previous day.

Dale and Shorty were the first to reach the fence and only had one cow and calf. When Holly and Emily showed up with eight or ten cows and calves, Emily teased Dale and Shorty. "Who brought the cow and who brought the calf?" she asked.

"I brought the cow," replied Shorty, before Dale could answer.

"But it's a pretty important cow and calf," said Dale. "The cow has the Grundy brand on her."

It wasn't long before the other riders started showing up with the cattle they'd gathered. Finally, late into the afternoon, Burkhart, Craig, Jimmy, and Tim showed up.

"Where's Bill?" asked Jimmy.

"I thought he was with you," said Emily.

"Well, he's missing," said Jimmy. "I'll have to go back and find him. Dale, you better come with me. There might be trouble."

"We'll start these cattle toward the gate, and when we get them through, we'll come and look for you," said Burkhart. "Don't you get lost!"

Jimmy and Dale started back to where Bill had last been seen. They found Bill about forty-five minutes later. He was having a hard time trying to keep a blind cow headed in the right direction. Without any cows to follow, she kept going around in circles. Bill couldn't keep her headed correctly.

When Jimmy saw the situation, he was greatly relieved. He had feared Bill had gotten into trouble and maybe hurt himself.

"You're okay?" asked Jimmy.

"Yep," replied Bill. "I think this cow is blind. She doesn't want to go where she's supposed to."

"I think you're right," replied Jimmy. "We better leave her and come back with the truck and trailer to get her."

"But Mister Burkhart said to bring everything," said Bill.

"I think he'll understand when he knows the story," replied Jimmy. "We'd better head back. Everyone is concerned."

They started back to where they'd left Burkhart and the others. They met them coming back to look for them.

When Jimmy explained the situation to Burkhart, Burkhart gave Bill a look of appreciation and improved respect. "You did a good job!" he told Bill.

"I figured we'd bring the truck and trailer out tomorrow and take her back to the ranch" said Jimmy.

"We might just as well shoot her where she is," said Burkhart.

"We can't do that," said Jimmy. "She's a Grundy cow! She'll make good hamburger for the ranch."

"That's your decision," said Burkhart. "I counted the cows through the gate. We're still short about thirty cows. But we'll bring the truck and trailer out tomorrow and haul her in. We might have a problem loading her, will you be along to help?"

"Sure," said Jimmy, before Shorty had a chance to answer.

The next day, the crew showed up at Burkhart's, early as usual. When they got there, they found Burkhart ready. Louise was to follow the riders to where they could load the cow in the trailer.

When they got to where the cow was, Burkhart roped the cow, took Jimmy's rope, tied it to his and took the end into the trailer, ran it around the frame and came back. He dallied up.

"I'll have to drag her into the trailer. Be ready to close the gate when she gets in," said Burkhart.

Jimmy got off his horse, gave the reins to Emily to hold and got into position to close the gate. When Burkhart had the cow close to the trailer, she fell down.

"Dale," said Jimmy, "tail her up. We can't drag her into the trailer."

Dale got off his horse and tailed the cow up. She didn't want to step up onto the trailer so he lifted one front leg into the trailer. Burkhart continued to pull the cow and she went down again.

Dale tailed her up again, then put the other foot into the trailer. With Burkhart still pulling the cow, she went into the trailer and fell down. Jimmy quickly closed the gate, but not before Dale got into the trailer with the cow.

"I'll get the rope off," he said.

"Better hurry," said Jimmy. "She'll be on the prod when she gets up!"

Dale got the rope off and quickly got out the gate, but not before the cow got up and got her head outside the gate. Jimmy was pushing the gate shut with all he could muster and Dale turned and helped. When they felt the cow pull back, they released the gate just enough where the cow could move back into the trailer and closed the gate and latched it.

"Good job, fellers," said Burkhart. "I didn't think we'd get the rope off until she was dead."

"Looks like to me you almost killed her here," said Shorty.

"Almost," said Burkhart. "If you're going to make hamburger out of her, we'll just have Louise take her to the slaughter house while she's loaded."

"That's not necessary," said Jimmy. "We can handle it."

"The Missus and I discussed it last night."

"Your supper is in the crock pot," said Louise. "Emily, you know where everything is. You can serve supper. Do you want the whole cow made into hamburger?"

"Fine," said Emily.

"This sounds like a done deal," said Jimmy.

"It is," replied Burkhart. "Now let's see if we can find more cows."

As Louise pulled away in the truck, the riders started in a different direction. Even though it was later in the day, they were still missing some cows and it wasn't too late to start looking for them.

They found a few cows and calves that day, but not all they were out. As they took the cows to the hayfields, Burkhart told Jimmy, "Tomorrow we'll sort the calves off the cows and sort off your pairs. We have a few of the neighbor's cows, too. I'll call them, maybe they've got some of ours. Do you plan on wintering your cows at your place?"

"Yes," replied Jimmy. "We'll sort off some club calves for the boys to raise as 4-H projects, sort off some cull cows and see what happens."

"You're going to have to haul the kids into town for the 4-H club meetings, aren't you?" asked Burkhart.

"Nope," replied Jimmy. "We're going to start our own club."

"If there's anything I can do to help, let me know. We'll gather these cows in the morning and start sorting. There's no need to show up as early as you have been."

"That's good," said Jimmy. "These boys could use a little break. What time do you want us here?"

"Around eight should work."

Emily served supper in the Burkhart kitchen and after supper she started cleaning the dishes. "We can't leave this mess for Louise," she said. "Who wants to help?"

Everyone except Tim volunteered and the dishes were done promptly.

Riding back to the ranch, Jimmy told the boys, "Tomorrow we have a surprise for you."

"What's that?" asked Shorty.

"Rather than getting up at four-thirty, you can sleep in until your regular time, six o'clock."

"Good," said Shorty.

"I was just getting used to getting up at four-thirty," said Bill.

"You can still get up that early if you want to," said Jimmy. "But I think I'll take advantage of it."

The next morning after the chores were done, the group made a leisurely ride over to the Burkharts. Burkhart was in the saddle when he greeted them. "I've got the gates set, all we have to do is gather the cows and put them in the big corral."

They gathered the cattle. Holly made the comment, "Rounding up in the hayfield is a lot easier than gathering in the mountains!"

The cattle were gathered, but not without some mishaps. The boys tried to force the cattle into the corral too fast and some cows tried to escape. Tim's horse started out to head off the escapees as fast as he could go and Tim almost fell off. But he had a good hold on the saddle horn and managed to stay on with a little help from Burkhart.

Holly took off his coat and started waving it to try and get the cattle in the corral. His horse promptly bucked him off. Jimmy rode up to where Holly was getting up, laughing.

"You all right?" he asked.

Holly, still laughing, nodded his head affirmatively.

Assured that Holly was okay, he caught Holly's horse. When he gave the horse to Holly, he said, laughing, "Don't be getting off that way! You'll be teaching the horse bad habits!"

Burkhart saw what was happening to Tim and rode up alongside him and straightened him in the saddle. They gathered the escapees and managed to corral them all. When the gate was closed, Burkhart said, "Don't try to rush cattle when you're trying to corral them. Just take it slow and easy."

With Jimmy's urging, Tim went and thanked Burkhart for helping him.

"Now, turn your horses into this corral and we'll start sorting," said Burkhart.

"Take the bridles off and tie them on the saddle," said Jimmy.

Burkhart had a good set of corrals and he assigned a boy to each gate—one for calves, one for cows, one for the Grundy cattle, and one for the neighbor's cattle. "Jimmy," he said, "I'll bring out the cattle one at a time, tell you which pen each critter goes in and you follow them down the alley, making sure they get in the right pen."

Jimmy relayed the instructions to the boys and they took up their positions. Emily, seeing that all the positions were covered, said, "I'll go to the house and see if I can help Louise."

The sorting started and although there was some confusion and mistakes to begin with, the longer they did it, the better the boys became at it. Dale stayed horseback and helped sort out the boys' mistakes.

About noon, Burkhart decided to stop for the noon meal. As they approached the house, they found Emily and Louise sitting on the porch, having iced tea.

"Do you have them all sorted now?" asked Louise.

"Nope," replied Burkhart. "We're only about half done. We'll be done tonight."

"Supper will be ready about five," said Louise.

Emily said, "Louise told me our hamburger will be ready and frozen next week. All we have to do is go pick it up."

At dinner, Burkhart said, "We'll finish sorting this afternoon then move your cows and calves to a little holding pasture. You can come and get them in the morning."

"That'll be fine," said Jimmy. "Although before we take them home, we'll need to ride fence and make sure everything is okay."

"Anyway you want to do it," said Burkhart. "I'll come and help you get started and take them home."

"That's not necessary," said Jimmy. "I think we have some real cowboys here."

"I'll come anyway," said Burkhart. "There's some places in that holding pasture where cattle can hide out, I'll help you."

They moved the Grundy cattle to the holding pasture, then they rode back to the ranch. Along the way, Emily said, "I think Louise appreciated a little extra help cooking for this bunch. That's quite a chore when you're not used to cooking for more than two.

The next day, the group rode fence around the hayfields. Emily didn't come along, she stayed behind to start preparing meals. It was about ten in the morning when the boys showed up at Burkhart's. Burkhart was already in the holding pasture and pretty well had it gathered when the boys showed up.

"I figured you'd be here about now," he said. "I think I've about got everything, but I'll check that corner over there. Craig, do you want to come along?"

"Sure," answered Craig.

"We'll meet you at the gate," said Burkhart, as he and Craig left.

"Let's take them home, boys," said Jimmy. "Holly, you go ahead and open the gate, but hold everything until Mister Burkhart and Craig show up. These are our cows, so take it easy with them."

They started the small herd toward the Rehabilitation Ranch, and it wasn't long before Burkhart and Craig showed up pushing a cow and calf.

They took the small herd to the ranch and turned them loose on the hayfields. Burkhart accompanied them all the way, riding beside each boy for a spell, thanking each one for their help. Before he left, he thanked Jimmy profusely for his help.

"In the past, it's taken me a week or ten days to gather as many cattle alone as we got in three days! I really appreciate all of your help."

"The colder it gets, the less riding we'll be doing," said Jimmy. "When do you want us to bring back your horses?"

"There's no rush," answered Burkhart. "Anytime that's convenient for you. I didn't expect you to winter them."

They shook hands and Burkhart left.

That night, Jimmy called the sale barn to see when the next sale would be. He wanted to wean the calves and get them started on feed before he sold them. He also needed to give each boy a chance to pick out a club calf. He also called the 4-H club advisor to see when he would be available to come out and meet with the boys and explain the 4-H program to them. He thought Harold Turner might be of some help to the boys in selecting their calves.

Snow started to fall that evening. *Winter is on its way,* thought Jimmy.

The next morning, while the boys were grooming the colts, Jimmy called the BLM to make arrangements for them to come and pick up the colts. "Are the colts ready for adoption?" asked the BLM supervisor.

"Yes sir," replied Jimmy "They've all been gentled and lead well. They've all had their feet picked up, they've all been saddled and it shouldn't be much for their future owners to start riding them when they get old enough and big enough. You can come out and see when you pick them up. Each boy has his favorites and they'll be glad to show them off to you. You need to bring a halter and lead rope for each colt. We're a little short of equipment out here."

They agreed on a date to take the colts the following week. The following week, Harold Turner was also to show up, with a portable scale to weigh each calf.

Next week will be a different week, thought Jimmy. *It will break the monotony.*

The following day, they sorted the calves off the cows. Then Jimmy went through the cows and sorted off some obvious cull cows. They turned the cows back on the hayfields. Jimmy then went through the calves and cut out some heifers that he thought might make good replacements. He sorted off bigger framed heifers and he took a few more than the number of cows he'd culled out.

When the sorting was done, Jimmy put the boys to work digging post holes for a chute. They could then put the calves in the chute and ear tag them, then get a weight on each calf. Craig made the remark, "It's a lot easier digging when you have some help. You don't have as many holes to dig."

They nailed poles to the inside of the posts they set and soon had a chute made.

When Harold Turner showed up the following week, he had a portable scale. They placed the scale at the end of the chute they'd constructed.

Harold explained a little about 4-H and handed out record books to each one of the youngsters. Then he explained a little about picking out a club calf. "You want to pick out large-framed animals that will grow good and put on a lot of weight."

"How do you do that?" asked Bill.

"That's hard to do," said Harold. "Your best bet is to pick out large-framed animals, not knowing who their mothers are. Let's get started. Who's first?"

Craig volunteered and Harold accompanied him into the pen to select a steer. Craig made his choice and Jimmy roped him and dragged him into a separate corral. They then put the steer into the chute and onto the scale. They weighed him and put a numbered ear tag in each ear. Harold recorded the tag number, the weight, and Craig's name in his book. The steer was turned into a separate pen.

"Be sure to record your calf's tag number and weight in your record books," said Harold.

They went through the same procedure with each boy having a turn at selecting a calf. They all had a good laugh when Holly selected a heifer.

"Pick another one," said Harold. "There are no fat heifer classes."

Tim was the last one to select a calf. All the calves were pretty much the same size and within thirty pounds of each other in weight. Harold had a lot to do with that. His advice to the boys was well heeded.

The ear tagging being done, Harold hooked up the scales to his truck and prepared to leave. "Any questions?"

"How do we keep track of the money we spend when we don't have any money?" asked Shorty.

"You'd better go over that with Jimmy," said Harold. "I'll be back in about a month or six weeks to weigh the calves again and see how you're doing."

At supper that night, Jimmy explained how he was going to work the feed bills out. "You'll measure the amount of hay you feed each calf and the amount of grain you feed. I'll charge each one of you what you use. When you sell the calves in the fall, I'll deduct your feed bill from your check and the remainder is yours. Be sure to keep accurate records, or I'll charge you too much." Jimmy smiled at this thought. "What money is left over is yours. I'd suggest you bank it in town in a savings account. You think about it over the winter.

"Tomorrow, we'll start halter-breaking the calves. They need to learn everything we taught the colts, although they might be a little slower learning it. ”

"Do we have to pick up their feet?" asked Bill. He'd been kicked picking up a colt's foot and remembered it well.

Two days later the BLM showed up. The boys showed off how gentle the colts were and the BLM supervisor was impressed. Each one of the colts, except one, even loaded in the trailer. With some persuading, that colt stepped into the trailer.

"He'd have loaded into the trailer, but we don't have one for the colts to become accustomed to," said Jimmy.

"I am impressed," said the BLM supervisor. "What's it been, about three months?"

"About that," replied Jimmy.

"When do you want some more?" asked the BLM man.

"Next week wouldn't be too early," said Jimmy.

"The boys have done a good job with these colts. How many more do you want?"

"Maybe twelve, replied Jimmy. "No, that's too many. Each boy has a club calf to care for. Eight will be plenty. That'll be two for each boy. We'll be able to keep them busy all winter with that number."

"I'll see what I can do, although next week might be pushing it a little. The following week might be better," said the BLM man.

"Whenever you say," said Jimmy. "We'll be ready for them. Better bring a halter and lead rope for each colt. We'll return them when you pick up the colts. It wouldn't hurt if you brought a little grain for the colts to help them through the winter."

"I'll see what I can do,'

The BLM supervisor drove off with the colts, obviously well pleased.

Dale approached Jimmy. "With the cattle gathered and the colts gone, I guess I'll be heading out for warmer temperatures."

"Well, I need to thank you for your help," said Jimmy. "I wish we could pay you something."

"I worked for room and board and a chance to help out if I could," replied Dale. "I've been well paid."

They shook hands and each one said, "Be seeing you around sometime. Take care of yourself."

Dale followed the BLM truck out to the highway. Emily drove her car out to where Jimmy was standing watching Dale follow the BLM truck.

"I'm going to town to get our hamburger," she told Jimmy. "Anything you need?"

"Nope," replied Jimmy.

As Emily drove off, Jimmy, noting that both Emily and Dale had left, wondered if there was anything going on between them. *I'll find out if she doesn't return,* he thought.

Jimmy noticed that all of the boys were almost in tears when the colts left. Shorty was fighting hard to hold back the tears, as were Holly and Bill. Craig and Tim didn't show any emotion.

"Don't get too attached to your calves," said Jimmy. "Or the new colts when they arrive. They'll all be gone before any of you boys are ready to leave. That's our job here, just to gentle them down for their future owners. You've all done a good job with them and are to be congratulated. Now, let's get back to teaching the calves something."

Emily returned later that day and had the boys help her put the hamburger in the freezer.

Winter came with a blast. Jimmy woke one morning to find a foot of snow on the ground. *We'll need some more equipment to handle this,* thought Jimmy.

The boys were up and getting ready for breakfast when he walked into the bunkhouse. "Make sure you clean your feet off real good before you go in the kitchen," he warned the boys. "We don't want to get the cook mad at us!"

Emily was on the porch when the boys arrived at the kitchen. "There's a broom here on the porch. Clean off your boots good," she told the boys as they arrived at the kitchen.

As Jimmy approached, Emily said, "Isn't it beautiful?"

"You won't think beautiful when you see how much of it is tracked into the kitchen!" replied Jimmy.

"I've already handled that," she said. "You can use the broom to clean off your feet, just like the boys!"

"Oh!" said Jimmy. "Thank you!"

After breakfast, Jimmy sent the boys to the barn to catch and tie up the calves. While they were doing this, Jimmy called the sale barn to make arrangements to get a truck to haul the calves and five cull cows to the sale.

When he got the sale barn, he asked, "When can you have a truck here to haul our calves and five cull cows to the sale?"

"Our next sale is Saturday. The only free time available is on Thursday morning."

"That will work," said Jimmy.

"Where are you?" asked the lady on the other end of the line.

Jimmy gave her instructions to the ranch. Then he asked, "What time will you be here?"

"Our driver should be there by eleven."

"Good," said Jimmy. "I want them on plenty of feed and water until the sale."

"What name do you want the check made out to?"

"Make the check out to the Rehabilitation Ranch. A Mister Mason from the probation department will pick it up," replied Jimmy.

"Is this Mister Mason on probation?" asked the lady.

Jimmy laughed. "No," he said. "He's the probation officer."

The lady, obviously embarrassed, asked, "Will he have identification papers?"

"Yes, and you can ask for them," said Jimmy still laughing.

Jimmy then called Mason and asked him if he could pick up the check and handle the brand inspection on Saturday.

"Sure," answered Mason. "What are you laughing at?"

Jimmy related his conversation with the lady at the sale barn. Mason even laughed a little himself.

As Jimmy went down to the barn to see how the boys were doing, he was surprised to see Burkhart driving in the yard on his tractor. There was a blade attached to the front end of the tractor.

"Kinda cold to be out on the tractor, isn't it?" he asked Burkhart.

"I dressed for it," replied Burkhart. "Thought I might move a little of this snow around for you. Where do you want me to start?"

"Anywhere you want," said Jimmy. He knew it was impossible to prevent Burkhart from plowing the snow, especially since he came over from his place on an open tractor.

"Better come in and have a cup of coffee and warm up before you start," said Jimmy.

"I could do that," said Burkhart.

"Keep the coffee hot, Emily. Richard Burkhart is here to plow snow, but he'll warm up some before he starts."

Burkhart entered the kitchen making sure he cleaned off his boots well.

"Louise has trained you well," said Emily, as he entered the kitchen. "Here's a cup of fresh coffee," she said, handing him a cup.

"Louise suggested I come over and move some snow," he said.

"You tell Louise we really appreciate it."

"It's the least I can do for all the help Jimmy and the boys were when hauling hay and gathering cows," said Burkhart.

"When you get done and before you leave, come in again and have a cup of coffee and warm up," said Emily.

After drinking a cup of coffee, Burkhart started plowing snow out of the yard. When he was done, he went to the house to get another cup of coffee.

While he was in the house, Jimmy came in. "Tomorrow we'll return your horses in the morning. I'll have Emily bring the truck to haul the saddles back. She'll have to make two trips, but she can do it."

"If you want, Emily, you can keep your horse, Rembrandt. You can keep him here over the winter. You might be able to ride some on better days," said Burkhart.

"That's mighty nice of you, Richard, but I don't think …"

"She'll keep him," interrupted Jimmy. "We have plenty of feed and she might feel the need to get away occasionally."

"That's a done deal," said Burkhart.

The next morning, Jimmy and the boys saddled their horses and rode to Burkhart's. "This will be the last ride you boys have until spring," said Jimmy. "Better enjoy it while you can. We'll see about getting some more horses in the spring."

Emily was already at Burkhart's when the boys arrived. They unsaddled the horses and put the saddles in the back of the truck.

"You take two boys and I'll take the rest in the Missus car," said Burkhart. "It'll save you having to come back."

"But you don't have to do that," said Emily.

"I know, but I'm going to!"

Thursday came and Jimmy and the boys had the calves ready to load. The truck showed up about ten-thirty.

"You're early," said Jimmy, as the driver climbed out of the truck. Seeing the loading chute, he'd backed the semi-trailer up to it.

"Better early than not at all," said the driver.

"We're ready for you, anyway," said Jimmy. "There are five cows, where do you want them?"

"We'll put them on the rear," said the driver.

They loaded the calves, some on the upper deck and some in the lower deck.

The driver asked if there were any special instructions. Jimmy said there weren't.

"The lady at the sale barn knows what to do with the check. Mister Mason can handle the brand inspection."

The truck driver got in the truck and without another word, left.

The next two weeks were spent gentling down the calves and oiling the saddles and leather equipment. One afternoon, Emily came down to the barn.

"The BLM supervisor called," she said. "They want to know if we can take eight head of weaner colts tomorrow."

"Of course we can," said Jimmy. "What did you tell them?"

"I told them we could. They'll be here around noon, depending on road conditions."

"Good," said Jimmy. "We'll be ready for them."

The next day, around one o'clock, the BLM truck arrived with eight head of weaner colts. They unloaded them in the corral. Jimmy looked them over and decided they had been weaned about a month earlier. But they all looked good, no lameness or serious conformation faults among them.

"Sorry I'm late," said the driver. "Road conditions on the other side of the mountain aren't the best. There's some grain in the back of the truck."

"That's okay," said Jimmy. "We're ready for about anything here, anytime. Boys, get the grain and put it in the barn."

Jimmy signed for the colts and the BLM driver drove off.

"We'll give them a day or two to settle down," said Jimmy. "Then we'll start gentling them. We'll do it the same way we did the others. You boys can tell Tim what we did with the first bunch."

Jimmy went to bed that night contented. In his mind, the Rehabilitation Ranch was a success. The juvenile delinquents had successfully halter-broke eight mustang colts and they had been returned to the BLM. They had helped Burkhart haul hay, gather and sort cattle. They'd learned how to saddle and ride horses. They had 4-H club calves started as a winter project. And, they had a second bunch of BLM mustang colts to halter-break and gentle. They had enough hay to winter over what was left of the Grundy cattle, the few horses they had, the mustang colts, and the club calves. They also were expecting a check from the sale barn for the sale of the calves and five cull cows.

"Yes," said Jimmy, out loud to himself, "the Rehabilitation Ranch is a success!" How much improvement the boys had made, he wouldn't be able to measure for quite some time. Only time would tell.

THE END

Other Books by Stu Campbell

Horsing Around a Lot

Horsing Around the Dudes

Humor Around Horses

You Can't Be Serious!

Comedy Around the Corral

More Humor Around Horses

Muddy Waters

A Young Cowboy's Adventure Series

A Young Cowboy's Adventure
Honey
Surprise!
Intruders
Expectations
Frozen
Advice
Broken
Ginny

Wild Horses for Wild Kids